I0548755

CAROLINE

By Sue Barr

Published by: Susan L Barr
Print ISBN: 978-0-9947718-5-8
Cover Design by Midnight Muse
Text copyright ©2017 Susan L. Barr
All Rights Reserved

This story would not be possible without the wonderful works of
Jane Austen and her book, Pride & Prejudice

Dearest Rob
You will <u>always</u> be my Mr. Darcy
I love you more than black jellybeans

Chapter One

Caroline Bingley descended the grand staircase and proceeded toward the breakfast room, barely acknowledging the footman who efficiently pulled a chair away from the table for her. With a soft swish of silk, she settled on the seat. When the second footman poured some tea, she deigned to give him a slight nod of approval, but that was because she was in a fine mood.

She noted through the window overlooking her sister's favorite garden that it was a beautiful Autumn morning, the leaves of the oak trees a riotous flame of red and orange. October was just around the corner and her good mood, which had been in evidence since late August, showed no sign of wavering. She'd even gone to church the day prior for mass and enjoyed the hymns, although the bishop nearly bored her to tears.

As she fussed with her morning meal, she mentally ticked off plans she and her brother had for the upcoming week. Charles had papers to sign with their lawyer to quit the lease at Netherfield Park and she had a fitting with Madam Beaufort before the much anticipated Annual Michaelmas Ball at Lady Addleworth's mansion.

Mr. Fitzwilliam Darcy was sure to attend the ball. He and his cousin, Colonel Fitzwilliam, who'd arrived in Town the other day, were spending an inordinate amount of time with Charles. She hoped it was because Charles finally decided to pursue an arrangement with Miss Georgiana Darcy. Darcy and the good Colonel, as her guardians, would finalize the articles of marriage as well as details of the dowry. With luck Charles would announce their engagement before the ball and with his shy little sister taken care of, Mr. Darcy could finally concentrate on his own happiness.

At last Charles was safe from Miss Jane Bennet, although he'd been reminded of her when they had the misfortune of running into her sister Elizabeth at Pemberley this past August. For a few days she'd worried Darcy might continue to grow in affection for the well-tanned miss with muddy hems and 'fine eyes', but fortunately she exited Derbyshire rather abruptly the very next day. Caroline did not need the ever-present Miss Bennet to ruin her plans for Charles and Georgiana as well as those for herself. After three long years of careful planning, she would not be denied her future by a girl of little consequence.

How she longed to be Mistress of Pemberley. To have others look to her for guidance, to run the household the way it should. First order of business would be to dismiss Mrs. Reynolds. The housekeeper was by far too smug and too familiar with Mr. Darcy. In fact, she let anyone who knocked on the door run amok within the house and on the grounds. Such behavior would cease the minute she and Mr. Darcy exchanged vows. Pemberley needed a strong hand to run efficiently and she had the fortitude to make it happen.

She bit into a light-as-air croissant and sighed. This was her only indulgence, otherwise the dress Madame Beaufort designed would never fit and she needed to look spectacular the night of the ball. Darcy would propose before night's end or her name wasn't Caroline Anastasia Bingley.

Their butler, Hobson, entered the room with a slight bow and signaled the footmen to remove the food trays. A light frown creased her forehead. Her sister Louisa took breakfast in bed and Mr. Hurst rarely awakened before noon, but surely Charles would be annoyed if he came down and there were no sausages and eggs readily available.

"Has Mr. Bingley been down to break his fast?"

"No, Miss. He left at first light with Mr. Darcy."

"Mr. Darcy?" Astonished, she set down her tea cup. "Did he state where they were going?"

"I believe he said they were going to Hertfordshire, ma'am."

Laden with heavy trays, the footmen exited the room and with another slight bow the butler followed.

"Hertfordshire," she mused aloud. "Why on earth would they go to Hertfordshire?"

Her mind whirled with possibilities. Charles may have decided to complete a final inspection of Netherfield Park before signing over the lease. She gave her head a quick shake at the thought. They had a perfectly good steward who took care of those details. And why would Darcy attend with him? Puzzled, she finished her croissant and tea before daintily dabbing her mouth with a linen napkin upon completion.

First thing, before attending her fitting, she'd write her

brother a letter and remind him of his duties and engagements in London. The last thing she needed was for Charles to inadvertently come across the ever amiable and angelic Miss Jane Bennet. Although convinced his desires no longer lay in that direction, she did not want to take the chance he might second guess his decision to quit Netherfield Park and Hertfordshire for good.

She took small comfort in the fact Darcy was along for the journey. If anyone could keep Charles from becoming entangled with a family of no social standing, and with the silliest of women in all of England for a mother, it would be Darcy. After all, it was he who helped convince her brother marrying Jane Bennet would have been social suicide, and not a moment too soon. After the ball at Netherfield, Charles was clearly besotted and it took the whole next day to convince him Jane Bennet did not have the same regard for him. Based on the mother's words and actions, her eldest was nothing more than a beautiful fortune hunter.

Satisfied all would be well, Caroline left the morning room and made her way to an ornate escritoire. Within minutes she'd penned a quick missive, sanded and blotted the heavy personalized vellum and skimmed the contents to make sure she hadn't missed a thing.

Grosvenor Street, London
September 14, 1812

Dearest Charles,

How wonderful you are attending Netherfield Park one last time before quitting it. Make sure you have not left a stray cravat lying about.

I am but teasing, sweet brother. However, I do want to remind you in the most loving way possible, of your appointment with our solicitor this Thursday. As well, Lady Addleworth's Annual Michaelmas Ball, which isn't until the following Tuesday, but there is much to do beforehand. Where would you be if I did not attend to your social calendar? I am so looking forward to this event as every one of our friends shall be in attendance. This will be a grand affair.

Hoping this letter finds you in good health. Give my warmest regards to Darcy.

Your loving sister,
Caroline

She sealed and addressed the letter before handing it off to Hobson for mailing. Satisfied her subtle direction would nudge Charles home quickly, she called to have a carriage brought round. Nothing and no one would interfere with her carefully laid plans.

Later in the week…

"Has my sister risen from her bed?" Caroline asked Hobson before handing her pelisse and gloves to her maid, Lucy. She'd returned from visiting Miss Miranda Blake, a thin scrap of a woman she'd met a few weeks prior through their mutual acquaintance, Miss Grantley. Miss Miranda's father was only a Baron, but every step into higher circles of Society brought her closer to becoming Mrs. Darcy of Pemberley. Her social resume would be impeccable when he finally proposed.

"She is in the front parlor."

"Lucy, lay out the dress we agreed upon for tonight. I shall be dining with Baron Blake's family and want no wrinkles in the skirt this time."

"Yes, Miss." Lucy gave a polite curtsy and proceeded upstairs with Caroline's pelisse and gloves.

"Have Bentley bring in some tea and cakes," she told Hobson, who'd closed the front door and now waited for her to leave the foyer.

"Yes, Miss."

Without a word of thank you, or even a polite nod at their long-time servant she breezed into the parlor. Louisa remained seated on a heavily tufted chair by the fireplace, her feet propped up on a small stool.

"Ah, Caroline. You have come home at last. I was dreadfully bored."

"Good afternoon, Louisa." Caroline settled on the settee across from Louisa. "I hope you do not mind, I asked Bentley to bring in tea."

"That is fine, dear. You always think of everything." Louisa slouched back against the chair with a huge sigh. "La, I am exhausted. I arose but an hour ago."

"You have been exhausted a lot, as of late," Caroline observed, noting the slight pallor of Louisa's complexion. "You may want to stay home a few evenings this week. You look like a washed-out rag."

"What, and miss all the fun? As you know, Mr. Hurst and I attended a dinner party hosted by the Marquis of Dorchester." Louisa sat erect and leaned toward Caroline. "He gave us a tour of his home and I saw his coronet!"

"How droll, Louisa. As if I care about a ceremonial hat."

"Do not put on your airs with me." Louisa said, a mutinous look crossing her face. "I know for a fact you have been vying for an invitation to one of his soirees for months."

Caroline bit the inside of her cheek to keep from retorting. Everything Louisa stated was true, but pride demanded she maintain a semblance of ennui. If she wished to move among the *ton*, she needed to emulate their disdain for anyone beneath them.

"Enough of the Marquis, have you heard from Charles? He did not attend his lawyer's appointment this morning."

"No, I have not, but then Charles is terrible at keeping Mr. Hurst and I in the know of his comings and goings." She picked out a sugared candy from the bowl on the table beside her chair and bit into it. Around the candy, she mumbled, "Do you know where he is?"

"Did I not tell you? How remiss of me. He went to Hertfordshire with Darcy."

"Hertfordshire!" Pieces of candy flew out of Louisa's mouth, which she quickly brushed off her lap onto the carpet. "Why on earth would they go there?"

"I do not know. They left this past Monday." Caroline eyed the half-chewed sticky mass on the floor and with great determination turned her focus back to Louisa. Not for the first time she wished her sister would not speak with her mouth full. In front of the wrong person, she could be mistaken for an uncouth gentlewoman, on par with Mrs. Bennet. "Lord knows there is nothing there except cows, chickens and those who tend them. I almost burst into song the day we shook the dust of Hertfordshire and Meryton off our shoes."

"He probably inspected Netherfield Park one last time.

You know how he loved that house."

Neither of them needed to add he'd loved more than the house at Netherfield.

"Yes, he did, but why has he not written back?" Caroline ignored an internal twinge at the reminder of how despondent their malleable brother had become and the unspoken reason why. "I sent a missive as soon as I learned of their departure. Surely he has received it by now."

"He and Darcy may have gone on to Pemberley, intending to return the day of the ball," Louisa offered hopefully. "It's a two-day trip from Hertfordshire to Derbyshire. Not much time to draft and post a letter and we all know how Charles abhors writing."

"What you say is true." Caroline stood and paced toward the window. She barely noticed the busy street with grand carriages parading up and down. Her mind was troubled by Charles' lack of response. What if he hadn't gone to Pemberley and instead tarried in Hertfordshire? The longer he dallied, the more apt he was to stumble across Miss Jane Bennet and that could be disastrous.

She turned at the rattling of a tray and watched as Bentley lowered the ornate silver tea set onto the small table in front of the couch. With a slight bow he took his leave, closing the door carefully behind him.

"Come, Caroline," Louisa said as she poured tea into their waiting cups. "We'll find out soon enough what Charles has been up to. Until that time, let me tell you who was at the Marquis' dinner."

Chapter Two

The arrival of a carriage alerted Nathanial Kerr that his anticipated guest finally arrived. He rose from his desk to meet the gentleman whose wedding he would be officiating a little over three weeks. The tall form of Mr. Fitzwilliam Darcy came up the front path and he hurried outside to greet his friend and patron.

"Darcy, I am so glad to see you again. It has been several months since we last spoke."

"I have had an interesting year. I assume you received my missive?"

"Yes, on Friday by express post. May I congratulate you on your upcoming nuptials?"

"Thank you." Darcy hastened them to enter the parsonage. "I will not dissemble, Kerr, I wish to have a word with you before Mr. Bingley arrives."

Filled with much curiosity, he guided Mr. Darcy to his study where the interview was slated to take place. The strange nervousness which the Master of Pemberley exhibited was intriguing, to say the least. As soon as they were safely in the privacy of his study Mr. Darcy began without preamble.

"What I have to say is a bit distasteful and I hope you will not be offended by my choice of language as I do not have much time. Bingley will be here in but a few moments." He paced to the fireplace and then turned to face Nathan. "I have kept your family connections secret from my fiancé's family. There are a few members who have a proclivity to…behave in somewhat vulgar manner. Of Mr. Bingley's family, I cannot say."

"Are you sure that is necessary, Darcy? I have never sought to hide my family connections although I must admit none of my – your – parishioners, with the exception of Mrs. Crenshaw, have knowledge of my title. I simply introduce myself as Mr. Kerr."

"Sadly, yes. Miss Bennet and Miss Jane will be told as they are both full of good manners and not given over to hysterics… I am sorry, Kerr. This is beneath me to complain."

They both turned when Mrs. Crenshaw, Nathan's housekeeper, knocked on the door.

"Mr. Bingley's arrived, Mr. Kerr." She bobbed a quick curtsy to Mr. Darcy and backed out of the room.

Charles Bingley strode into the room and Nathan immediately like the pleasant young man. He was a perfect foil to Mr. Darcy's quiet nature. After introductions were made, sans title, the men quickly took their places and began discussing the upcoming joint weddings. After about an hour, Nathan set down his quill with satisfaction. He rested his gaze on Mr. Darcy.

"The banns will be read over the next three Sundays and I

am honored to preside over the wedding ceremony of you and Miss Bennet, and" – he turned his gaze to Mr. Bingley – "you and Miss Bennet the first of November."

Both men looked at each other and smiled. Of all his duties, weddings were fast becoming his favorite. This one, for his benefactor and patron, was particularly special.

"When you offered me this living three years ago, Mr. Darcy, I had hoped this day would come. Your father, were he here, would be overjoyed at your finding a woman who brings you much contentment."

"I very nearly missed her," Darcy said. "I thank God daily He allowed me to see the folly of my ways and mend them. Elizabeth – Miss Bennet – will be a good helpmate with my estate and a true sister to Georgiana."

"I am inclined to agree with you. From what you have stated, she and her sister, Miss Jane Bennet are most amiable. I believe both of you will have long and prosperous marriages."

"True words, Kerr. My hope is that one day you will find a woman who will compliment your position here, in Kympton."

"I pray you are right, Mr. Darcy," Nathan stated with a slight smile. "Only the good Lord knows who would be a fitting companion for a vicar such as I. Not everyone is as lucky in love as you two." He glanced down at his notes. "The ladies are in agreement with the ceremony taking place here instead of near their home?"

"I know Louisa and Caroline, my sisters," Bingley offered as explanation, "would prefer our weddings to take place in London, but Pemberley seemed the most appropriate choice. If it were not for Darcy, my Jane and I might never have reconnected." Mr. Bingley turned to his friend with a large grin. "He will not allow me to thank him properly, but I have no hesitation in declaring Mr. Darcy as the truest of friends."

"Bingley, you give me too much credit." Darcy gave a small wave of his hand as if fending off his effusive compliments. "Pemberley is the obvious choice because our chapel is larger than the one in Meryton and we will have three families attending the ceremony. Please do not read anything more into it than that."

Nathan watched the two men banter back and forth, their easy friendship such a blessing. He and his brothers shared such a comradery, at least when they weren't trying to best each other. Nothing was off limits in their quest to win. They even went so far as to holding a spitting contest. Which would not have been so bad, but their target had been their mother's favorite vase.

She'd arrived in the sitting room to find a priceless Ming vase covered with tiny, wet, sticky wads of paper. Their punishment had been to polish all the silver in the house and after 'the incident' as it became known, all of them agreed Mother's things were off limits.

But for the most part, the brothers kept their more spirited adventures outdoors. Nanny had her hands full mending cuts and bruises, not to mention a few broken bones.

All came to an end when Maxwell went off to Eton, followed by George the following year. A long two years elapsed before Nathan joined them and by that time Max was preparing for Cambridge. Yet, the brothers remained close, more so when their father died late last year and his title fell to their eldest brother. At eight and twenty, Max never expected to become a Duke.

Nathan was grateful for Mr. Darcy's offer to become vicar of his family's church at the village of Kympton, a short distance from Pemberley Estate. After resigning his commission he'd no desire to remain in London. At the time, as the son of a Duke, he'd have been invited into many great homes, but his heart lay in a humbler direction and near the end of his seminary studies, Darcy approached him. Because Darcy attended Cambridge with Max, he knew Nathan was in want of a good living.

"Is there anything more you require, Mr. Kerr?" Darcy asked, breaking into his thoughts.

"I would like to meet with the young ladies and have a discussion with them to assure myself, and the Church of England, they are indeed ready for the great adventure which lies before them."

"I believe you wrote earlier you have business to attend in London next week." Nathan affirmed with a quick nod. "Then I will arrange something during that time. Elizabeth and Jane will be in Town for their trousseau fittings and a quick interview can be arranged at their Uncle's home."

"Excellent. I look forward to meeting them both."

All three men rose and made their way outside. A gleaming black coach with the Darcy coat of arms on the door and four matching greys waited. Darcy himself may not have a title, but his noble heritage ran deep and long, going back even further than Nathan's and there were enough Earls and Viscounts in the family line to satisfy an inspection of Debrett's Peerage by ladies of the *ton*.

"Good day to you, Mr. Kerr," Darcy said as he entered the carriage. Bingley swung up on his horse and waited. "I shall have my steward come around with a date and time for you to meet our brides as well as the Gardiner's address." He closed the door and tapped the carriage roof to let the driver know he could proceed.

Nathan gave him a courteous nod and watched them leave. He could not wait to meet the woman who'd captured the elusive, very private Mr. Darcy. She seemed a paragon of virtue and if there was one thing he knew to be true, Mr. Fitzwilliam Darcy did not give compliments easily. Nor censure. The fact he worried enough about the behavior of his betrothed's family to give warning made Nathan pause for a moment.

He shook his head and re-entered the parsonage. He'd survived the panting mothers of Society and the wiles of many a deceptive debutante, surely, he could handle the bride's family with ease.

~~~ooo0ooo~~~

"I am so glad you are home. I have some news."

Caroline glanced up as Louisa entered the front parlor and took a seat across from her. Mildly surprised at her sister's abrupt entrance, she set down the pillow she'd been stitching.

"Whatever is the matter? You look positively flushed." Caroline picked up the tiny bell on the table beside her and rang for tea.

"I have received a letter from Charles—"

"Finally! He missed his lawyer's appointment as well as Lady Addleworth's ball. I do not think I can ever forgive him for leaving me without a dance partner."

"Never mind the ball; he has done something absolutely dreadful."

Without another word, Louisa pulled a letter from her

pocket and handed the crumpled piece of paper to Caroline. She glanced at the front of it to see when the letter had been posted.

"This was mailed almost a week ago." She tried to smooth the single sheet out and held it to the light coming from the front window. "No wonder it took so long to arrive, the address is smudged. His penmanship has not improved."

Charles had a tendency to run his sentences together and large ink smudges concealed a few words, but not all.

"His penmanship is the least of our worries."

Raising an eyebrow at her sister's caustic tone, Caroline attempted to read her brother's hasty scrawl.

Hertfordshire, Netherfield Park
October 2, 1812

"He has not quit Netherfield Park!" She exclaimed when she saw the date and place Charles wrote from.

"Again, dear sister, that is the least of our concerns. Read on!"

Without bothering to look up at her sister, whom she knew was most likely gritting her teeth in anger, she continued reading.

Dearest Louisa,

I write you with the most wonderful news. Mr. Darcy and I attended Netherfield Park a few weeks ago and as they were a particular acquaintance of ours, we paid a visit to the Bennet family of Longbourn. We were graciously received and delighted to be invited to dine, en famille.

I will not keep you in suspense, dear sister. Miss Jane Bennet has accepted my offer of marriage. We are to be wed as soon as the banns are read. Mr. Darcy graciously invited dear Jane and me to be married the same day he and Miss Elizabeth exchange their vows. The ceremony will take place the first day of November at Pemberley.

I remember how much you liked Jane. You and Caroline stated she was a sweet girl, which she is, and she looks forward to being a loving sister to both of you. I am the happiest man in all of England. Nay, all the world.

I shall return to London once Darcy and I have finalized details with the vicar at Kympton.

Your loving brother,
Charles

The letter fell from Caroline's fingers onto her lap. How could this happen? She'd worked so hard cultivating a friendship with Darcy, making sure she never stepped outside the bonds of polite society. She'd carefully selected friends amongst those who would advance their social status once married. Had all of it been in vain?

"Caroline? Are you quite well?"

"What?" She shook out of her dazed thoughts at her sister's concern and stared at her.

"I asked if you were—"

"Yes, yes. I am fine." She jumped to her feet, ignoring the pillow that fell to the floor and began to pace. "How could Darcy propose marriage to…to…"

"A woman he thinks quite handsome?"

"NO!"

Her heart could not stand the thought of Darcy finding

Miss Elizabeth Bennet more handsome than she. Eliza Bennet wore simple muslin gowns and walked for miles in mud, not caring what anyone thought. Her family teetered one step higher than tenant farmers. Her uncle lived in Cheapside on Gracechurch Street, of all places! Eliza Bennet was a low born nobody and marrying her would drag the Darcy name through the very mud she liked to cavort amongst. How could he do this to her?

"At least he will be happy." Louisa sounded almost weary and Caroline cut a quick glance at her.

Some sympathy coursed through her as she noticed pinched lines around Louisa's mouth and eyes. Life hadn't been easy for her. What should have been a great match to Mr. Hurst had turned sour when his character was revealed within the first year of marriage. He was a lazy man who liked nothing better than to spend Louisa's inheritance on drink and cards. All the more reason Caroline set her cap at Mr. Darcy. He never gambled, nor drank to excess. His estate was profitable and the mistress of Pemberley would want for nothing. All her plans were ruined. Eliza Bennet would now live the life she coveted with every fiber of her being.

"Come, Caroline. Drink your tea before it becomes cold. There is nothing we can do about it now."

She sank onto the settee, her hand to her chest as if constricted with an unknown pain. For the past year she'd subtly hinted to a chosen few of Darcy's fondness of her and how she expected him to come up to scratch in the near future. That he would marry *her*, Eliza Bennet...

She broke off the thought, yet her mind refused to heed her desires, racing in a multitude of directions, all of which led back to the fact her attendance at the wedding was mandatory. Crushed dreams or not, she must present a pleasant face or risk becoming the laughing stock of the *ton*. It was only after Louisa went to speak with Cook about the evening meal that Caroline paced the front parlor, alone with her thoughts.

What was it about the men in her life that they became addlepated over two country misses? Had they no sense at all? She blew out a frustrated breath and continued to pace.

She'd argued with her sister that although they would attend the wedding, there would be no convivial visits during Christmas. Louisa, the viper, pointed out they'd have to attend any and all christenings as Charles always wanted a houseful of children. At that statement she almost brought back up her tea.

She stopped pacing and clenched her fingers into a tight fist. Why hadn't Darcy kept Charles away from Jane, and more disturbing, why had he proposed to Eliza Bennet? If only Darcy and Charles had taken her with them, then neither would be marrying into that odious family.

Of that she was positive.

She pivoted from the window and sat on the settee near the fireplace. Her foot bumped something beneath the small couch and she pulled out the pillow she'd been stitching. Tension snaked through her body at the sight of her pitiful attempt to capture Pemberley in needlepoint.

She nearly tossed the unfinished reminder of her failure into the fireplace, instead, all her anger, frustration, all her tattered hopes and dreams coalesced into a fit of fury and she tore the pillow to shreds with her bare hands. Minutes later, fingernails broken and fingertips bruised, she threw the mangled mess to the floor. Great gasps racked her chest as she fell to the floor and sobbed.

"Caroline!"

She raised her head at the sound of Charles' voice and attempted to wipe away her tears with trembling fingers. He rushed to her side and helped her onto the settee. With an impatient huff she swatted his hands from her arms and turned her back to him.

"Go away, Charles. I am not fit company at the moment."

"I cannot leave you like this."

A fresh linen cloth was pressed into her hand and she used it to cleanse the tears from her face.

"I am sure you have more important things to do than sit with a sister who has lost all her composure."

Tears threatened to bubble up and flow down her cheeks once again. The settee shifted as Charles sat beside her, his shoulder bumping into her back, something he'd done when they were children.

"There is nothing I would rather do than comfort my sister when she is obviously in distress. Is there anything I can get you? Anything I can do to help you with…with, whatever this is?"

She turned slightly and glanced at him from the corner of her eye. His expression was sincere, with no hint of malice.

"Yes. Do not marry Miss Bennet."

Charles barked out a laugh and stood.

"That is something I will not do. I wasn't going to mention this, given my extreme happiness, but I discovered you knew Jane was in London this past January and kept that information from me." His brow furrowed slightly. "I have half a mind to cut your clothing allowance by half until you are well and truly married."

"You would not!"

"Do not push my good nature, Caroline. If my marriage to the most amiable woman in England is the source of your anguish, then I suggest you find ways to cope. Miss Jane Bennet is an angel and I intend to marry her as fast as humanly possible."

"But why, Charles?" Caroline sprang to her feet and faced him, the tear-stained linen cloth clutched against her chest. "We agreed before we quit Netherfield that she was not right match for you. What of Georgiana?"

"What *of* Georgiana?" he queried back, then his eyes narrowed and his body stiffened. "Did you think I was going to offer for Miss Darcy? She is but a child! Is that what 'this' is all about?" He indicated the shredded pillow on the floor.

"No," she answered swiftly with a shake of her head. His gaze hardened and she relented, "Yes, but there is more to my distress than what you think. I am not a complete ninny-hammer."

"Not from where I stand." He gave her a stiff bow. "I will see you at dinner. I hope by then you will be composed."

He exited the room and she fell back to the settee. How much worse could this day become?

"Oh, and Caroline…"

She sat more erect and glanced over her shoulder. Charles had returned and now stood in the doorway, his usually cheerful face dark with anger.

"…Darcy traveled with me to London as he has some business to attend and will dine with us this evening. Try to behave like a lady. Try to behave like my Jane would."

With that he turned and this time she heard him ascend the stairs, his rebuke ringing in her ears. For better or worse she had to face Darcy. She stood, drew in a deep breath and smoothed down her skirt. With a heartfelt sigh she went upstairs to repair the damage her temper had wrought.

Chapter Three

Caroline pulled the ivory lace gloves high upon her forearms and perused her hands. After trimming her nails almost to the quick and soaking them in rose water, her fingernails did not look as ghastly as they had earlier. She would have to remove the gloves to eat, but with Darcy seated to the right of Charles and she directly across from them, the two men would be none the wiser. Louisa might take notice, but as hostess she would be seated at the other end of the table, next to her husband and most likely would say nothing.

She descended to the first floor and made her way toward the drawing room. Familiar male voices carried out into the hall and for a moment she stopped and took a deep breath. How could she face Darcy, knowing he'd never be hers? She heard Charles laugh, followed by, "I say, Darcy. That vicar of yours is a fine man. He has a good sense of humor and will suit you and Miss Bennet admirably."

A sharp pain lanced through her heart. She did not know if she could face her greatest disappointment without bursting into tears. Words of her grandmamma seeped into her consciousness. *When in doubt, trust in the Lord. He has nothing but good things for you.*

Dear grandmamma, a hardworking tradesman's wife, spent much time in prayer, her worn out bible constantly by her side. She'd always known the right words to calm her headstrong granddaughter's heart and thoughts.

"Thank you, grandmamma," she whispered as she took a deep breath, squared her shoulders and swept into the room. Charles and Darcy stood by the fireplace and Mr. Hurst lounged in his favorite chair, a glass of port within easy reach. Caroline decided on a forthright approach and not let Darcy know how crushed she was by his asinine decision.

"My congratulations, Darcy, on your upcoming nuptials." She gave him a small curtsy in greeting.

"Thank you, Miss Bingley." He nodded his head in return, his expression inscrutable. Unnerved by his cool demeanor, she turned to her brother.

"What were you saying about Darcy's vicar, Charles?" She made her way to the settee and took her seat, mentally cringing in remembrance of the state her brother found her earlier.

"I was saying he is full of good humor." Charles moved toward the drink tray and poured a small sherry for her. She briefly wished he would give her a splash of bourbon or something stronger to calm her nerves, but she smiled and accepted the overly sweet drink. "He is nothing like I expected from a man of the cloth."

"How did you find him, Darcy?" She took a sip and shuddered when the ghastly concoction of sweetness hit her taste buds.

"I attended Cambridge with his brother. He knew I was

looking for a candidate as the position had been vacated by the untimely passing of Mr. Penfound. He contacted me and as soon as Mr. Kerr completed his seminary studies, I offered him the living at Kympton."

"How fortuitous for you. I know you wanted a good man there. Does he have a wife, children?"

"No, the vicar is a single man. There is no rush for him to enter the estate of marriage." Mr. Darcy took a sip of his drink. "But, I am sure when he does his wife will be extremely content."

This small talk gave her a headache. Frankly, she could care less who led the Darcy family through the gates of heaven. She only needed them to think she was happy with their dismal choices and move on in her life. She took another sip of her sherry, willing it to stay down. Charles and Darcy talked quietly for a few moments and she took advantage of their inattention to assess the situation.

The Earl of Matlock was Darcy's uncle and Darcy himself was on friendly terms with other members of nobility. The guest list had a distinct probability of being high ranking and very influential, which was fortuitous as she was in need of a new plan. At that moment, Louisa made her entrance and without further delay the party proceeded to the dining room.

~~~ooo0ooo~~~

"With the wedding being held at Pemberley, the Earl of Matlock can attend with ease. That must please you, Darcy." Caroline cut into her excellent salmon as she spoke across the table to Mr. Darcy.

"Both he and my Aunt, along with my cousins will travel down the day of the ball."

"The ball?"

"Yes. It's a longstanding Darcy tradition. We host a ball a few days prior to the wedding. As both Charles and I, along with our brides shall depart directly from the wedding breakfast, this is a chance for everyone to meet and become better acquainted in a less formal setting."

Caroline should have listened to the small voice of reason urging her to temper her words, but she still smarted over the set-down from Charles earlier in the day and spoke without thought.

"Are you quite sure your esteemed family is prepared to become better acquainted with your new in-laws, Darcy?"

She realized her error as soon as the words left her mouth.

"Those who cannot accept this marriage are not welcome at Pemberley, *Miss* Bingley." Darcy replied in tones cold enough to freeze the Thames. "Fewer table settings at our wedding breakfast will not make it a sad affair."

"Fortunately for us, Mr. Darcy," Louisa's voice carried down the table, "we shall be welcome at Pemberley for a long time as we adore the Bennet's."

Caroline gripped her fork tight. She hadn't missed Darcy's intentional emphasis on her proper title of 'Miss' Bingley.

"Most certainly, Louisa and I commented this very afternoon on what a sweet girl Jane Bennet is and how lively the conversations are when Miss Eliza is around."

She willed herself to smile and took a bite of her salmon, which felt and tasted like sawdust in her mouth. However enraged she was at these two fools becoming entangled with the Bennet family, she would not allow herself to act upon that anger. Her momentary loss of control this afternoon would not be repeated.

After the meal the ladies retired to the drawing room while Charles, Mr. Hurst and Darcy remained to enjoy a glass of port. Louisa fussed with her skirts after settling in her favorite chair. Caroline paced in agitation for a few minutes until Louisa implored her to sit.

"Sister, you shall wear out the tread in my new carpet, prowling around like a caged animal."

"I am sorry, Louisa. This evening has been most trying."

"Pull yourself together before the men join us. We have but a few minutes while they enjoy their port."

"You mean while they pat each other on the back over their most advantageous marriages." She flopped onto the settee, uncaring if the silk of her skirt became wrinkled and huffed out a sigh. "It is unconscionable what Charles and Darcy have done." Her heart squeezed a little tighter at the thought of Eliza Bennet being mistress of Pemberley in place of her. "What could I have done different?"

"Apparently, nothing. You never were and never will be a woman Darcy considered marrying. Cast your net on the other side of the boat, Caroline. There are other fish in the ocean."

Chapter Four

Caroline stabbed the quill into the ink pot and tapped off excess ink before poising the feathered pen over a blank sheet of paper. She knew she must make amends with Jane and heal the rift between herself and Charles. Several crumpled sheets later she finally penned a note meeting her approval.

Grosvenor Street, London
October 14, 1812

My dearest Jane

How delighted Louisa and I are at the thought of you becoming our sister. We knew, from the very first time we met in Hertfordshire, you were one of the sweetest girls ever to grace our home. Charles is ecstatic over your upcoming nuptials and we join him in the excitement.

We look forward to welcoming you to the family.

Affectionately, your sister
Caroline

The only good thing she found in this humiliation was the fact she did not have to placate Mr. Darcy and write a letter to *her*.

"Caroline?" She turned at the sound of her sister calling out her name.

"Oh, there you are." Louisa stopped in the doorway to the parlor. She was dressed for an afternoon outing and was in the act of pulling on her gloves. "I am off to Mrs. Pike's for tea. Do you care to join us, dear?"

"No, thank you. I have to finish this letter and post it immediately."

Understanding dawned on Louisa's thin face.

"Ah, yes. 'Tis good you are mending the tender bonds of fraternal love. At least *that* Sword of Damocles shall not hang over your head at the wedding. That is, if you can bring Jane around to loving us again."

"I will do my best, sister."

"Be grateful you do not have to apologize to Miss Elizabeth Bennet," Louisa chortled. "I shall see you this evening at dinner."

"Louisa!" She called her sister back.

"Yes?"

"Where did we go wrong? How did he fall into the clutches of the Bennet family?"

"I am going to assume you mean Charles and not Mr. Darcy." At her nod Louisa continued. "We underestimated his feelings. After almost a year he loved her still, if not more than when we quit Netherfield Park. No good will come from dwelling in the land of 'what if'. Reconcile with Jane and be done with it."

"It is not that easy. I cannot stand the fact they are throwing their lives away."

"I have come to terms with their upcoming nuptials. You are the only person in this family who objects to their marriages. Jane is a sweet girl and will make Charles happy and after that incident at Pemberley this past summer, Darcy only tolerated us for the sake of his friendship with Charles."

"What incident?" She could not stop the haughty tone permeating her words.

"Do not be obtuse. You know exactly what you did and you failed then as you have failed now. I have no time for a re-hashing of your grievances; I shall see you at dinner."

Caroline remained seated after Louisa departed, a bit shocked that her sister was aware of an embarrassing incident during their last visit to Pemberley in early August. The fact Charles relayed a portion of what occurred between her and Darcy was undeniable. That he'd not shared the complete truth was also undeniable. She turned her head sharply, raised her chin to the soft sunlight pouring through the window and closed her eyes tight, willing the tears which threatened to course down her cheeks to stay. She would rise above this. She had to.

$$\sim\sim\sim\text{ooo0ooo}\sim\sim\sim$$

The play was a roaring bore and Caroline stifled a small yawn behind her fan. The only thing which kept her from nodding off to sleep was the company they were in. The Marquis of Dorchester.

The Marquis had a private box at The Theatre-Royal – Covent Garden which seated six. Along with her family and the Marquis, the other two guests were Lady Susan Cruikshank and

Sir Reginald Slade.

To be in such esteemed company filled her with deep satisfaction. More than one lady and gentleman glanced their way throughout the evening making her glad she'd worn her newest gown, cut in the latest fashion in her favorite color of burnt amber. She learned long ago that given her red hair and green eyes, bold colors were needed to bring them to life.

If only the Marquis would cease doting on the non-descript Lady Susan, who paled in comparison to the wit and vivacity she brought to the party. Having been relegated to the back row of the private box with her sister and husband, she'd been unable to miss how the Marquis leaned intimately toward her ear during the performance, or how often Sir Reginald panted for attention from the other side.

What were they so enraptured by other than the fact she was titled? While Lady Susan's dress was excellently made, it was nothing more than a glorified day dress. All blues and white with small pink flowers embroidered along the hem. And the poor freckled face dear had no dowry what-so-ever to recommend herself with, only ten thousand pounds. A paltry sum when compared to her own twenty thousand. What *did* the insipid Susan Cruikshank have that she lacked?

The interval bell rang and the whole party made their way to the salon where refreshments were offered. She found herself on the arm of Sir Reginald, who almost broke into a trot in order to keep up with the Marquis. He, at least, escorted Lady Susan in a reasonable fashion, not pulling her along as though she were some child's toy.

When Sir Reginald tugged her arm once more in an effort to hurry her along, she decided she'd had enough of this dog and pony show and halted in the middle of the room near a large column. When her arm extended as far as it could go, she released his. He advanced a few more steps before realizing she was no longer attached, but rather, behind him.

"Miss Bingley?" He had the grace to look a bit embarrassed, though not for long. His head quickly swiveled in search of the Marquis and Lady Susan.

"Sir Reginald, may I wait for you here?"

"Yes, Miss Bingley." At his look of relief, she became piqued. Was her company that repellant? "I shall return post haste with some refreshing lemonade."

Before she could utter 'no thank you', or ask for something more bracing, he'd moved through the growing crowd toward the Marquis. Louisa and Mr. Hurst arrived and stood beside her.

"Your escort stranded you already?" Louisa queried with apparent glee. "Is he in love with Lady Susan as well?"

Caroline nodded in assent. Both Lord Dorchester and Sir Reginald were chasing the same fox. She'd seen this sort of besotted behavior with Charles when he first laid eyes on the angelic Miss Jane Bennet. If Lady Susan were smart, she'd keep the Marquis close and cut Sir Reginald loose. At least, that's what she would do.

Lord Dorchester had several estates, along with his house in London and appeared to have a nice steady income from his holdings. Yes, he would do nicely, if only he'd get his head out of the cloud of effervescent bubbles encircling Lady Susan long enough to notice her. Not for the first time she railed at the fact she'd spent three years pursuing Mr. Darcy. What a colossal waste of time that turned out to be.

"Caroline," Louisa interrupted her thoughts. "Do you see who is here?"

Her sister nodded in the direction of the refreshment area and Caroline craned her neck to see above the crowd. There were times when she was grateful for the extra few inches of height God deemed fit to bestow upon her.

"Whom are you speaking of?"

"The Duke of Adborough," she hissed. "I heard he arrived in London for the late Season. Many a frantic mama will be vying for his attention for their darling daughters. The poor man."

"Poor!" Caroline snorted, recognizing his name. "His duchy is more valuable than Darcy's estate. There is nothing poor about the Duke of Adborough."

"I meant the tigresses encircling the poor man, looking for an opening."

"Louisa, you have been reading too many adventure novels. Pray tell, which one is he?"

"There, he wears the deep blue and ivory redingote."

Caroline glanced over to where two men stood. Both were handsome in face and she should have been more attracted to the Duke, as he was single and in want of a good wife, but the other man with his dark tousled hair and broad shoulders caused a tiny rift of excitement to course through her veins. Never had she felt this way about a man and it was disconcerting.

She struggled to keep from staring, but her gaze returned to the two men time and time again. If only someone of consequence were here to introduce them, then maybe this small obsession with a person she'd never met would cease.

~~~ooo0ooo~~~

"You seem to have an admirer." Nathan said in a low voice to his brother.

"Dare I ask whom?" Max glanced around the room.

"A fiery vixen, standing near the column."

How could his brother not have noticed her? The minute she'd entered the room on Sir Reginald's arm, he'd been intrigued. When Sir Reginald abandoned her, he'd fought the urge to approach the mysterious siren who beckoned like a flaming ember in the midst of mediocrity. It was then he noted that she, and the lady standing beside her, showed a marked interest in Max. He may as well have been standing on the moon for all the notice sent his way.

Taking his time, Max glanced in their general direction and a grin threatened to break across his face. He swiftly turned so the young lady would not see.

"I think you need to have your eyes checked, brother. The beauty is not looking at me, but has her attention fixed upon you."

"What?" Nathan gave a start. He was unused to anyone paying him attention, at least not in London where Debrett's Peerage ranked alongside the Holy Bible as required reading. He cast another side long glance at the woman and noted that indeed she darted furtive glances his way.

"Adborough!"

Nathan and Max turned to see the Marquis of Dorchester approach, a young lady upon his arm with Sir Reginald close behind.

"Dorchester, what a pleasant surprise." Max gave the Marquis a polite nod.

"I heard you were back in Town. May I present my friend, Lady Susan Cruikshank, the Earl of Tenyham's daughter, and of course you both know Sir Reginald."

Lady Susan executed a perfect curtsy and Sir Reginald gave both brothers a polite nod.

"It is a pleasure to meet you, Lady Susan." Max said and turned to Nathan. "And this is my brother, Lord Nathan."

Nathan greeted them with all politeness and took note with some interest, the beautiful woman he and his brother discussed approached, the other lady and gentleman in tow. Dorchester detected them at the same time and hastened them over.

"Adborough, these are my acquaintances, Mr. and Mrs. Hurst and Mrs. Hurst's sister, Miss Bingley."

Nathan registered two things almost instantaneously. First, Dorchester introduced the three strangers as mere acquaintances where Lady Susan received the nod as a friend. Second, the name of the beauty was Bingley. What were the odds the two sisters were the very ones related to Mr. Bingley, friend of Mr. Darcy? Before he could comment, Mrs. Hurst dropped into a deep curtsy and upon rising tittered, "I am most honored to meet you, Your Grace."

Her supercilious tone grated. He'd seen this type of behavior toward their father his whole life and given Max's cool reception, he realized his brother was also aware of this fact.

The sister, Miss Bingley, noted their demeanor and her tone retained a more modest quality. "I am pleased to make your acquaintance, Your Grace." She turned emerald green eyes upon Nathan, her cheeks flushing a becoming shade of pink, "And you as well, sir."

At least Miss Bingley acknowledged him. The sister was apparently still too much in awe from meeting a Duke to greet him. He returned her curtsy with a polite bow and murmured. "The pleasure is mine, Miss Bingley."

Dorchester and his brother entered into a conversation about the latest happenings in Parliament and Sir Reginald focused his attention solely on Lady Susan, whose outward behavior was all politeness but not overly warm. Nathan deduced her charms were being saved for Lord Dorchester.

Mrs. Hurst listened with rapt attention to his brother's conversation while her husband removed himself to the refreshment area. He wished her luck in deciphering what they droned on about. Parliamentary business was a large pendulum which swung from the atrocious to the tedious.

He turned his attention to Miss Bingley, standing quietly beside him.

"Are you enjoying the play, Miss Bingley?"

"Yes. I have not been to the theater in such a long time I had forgotten how diverting they are."

"Have you been among savages, that you have not enjoyed the pleasures of London? Maybe a dangerous journey to the deepest, darkest jungle?"

Her reply was a combination of an elegant sniff and a cynical laugh.

"No savages, Lord Nathan, although it seemed that way at the time"

"Do you live in Town or are you here only for the Season?"

"I am with my sister and her husband at present. Our brother is purchasing an estate in Hertfordshire and I may impose myself on him in the future."

At the mention of Hertfordshire his assumption was solidified these two ladies were indeed Mr. Charles Bingley's sisters. About to comment he'd met her brother; the bell rang for the second half of the play.

"I must take my leave, Miss Bingley." He reached for her gloved hand and maintaining intimate eye contact, gallant bowed over her slender fingers. "I look forward to seeing you again."

In that instant he had the insane desire to kiss her inviting, full lips. Something in his demeanor must have relayed itself, because her eyes widened and she gasped softly. Ashamed by his physical reaction to a virtual stranger, he released her hand and straightened to his full height. There was a time in his life when he would have pursued her relentlessly, seeking only physical pleasure, but he was a new man and those ways were gone.

With a polite nod he left the group and waited for his brother in their private box. Inadvertently his eyes scanned the boxes until he found the Marquis' and watched Miss Bingley take her seat. Within seconds their eyes met across the theater and just as quick she averted her gaze to the stage and even though the distance was great, Nathan noted her cheeks flush.

Without a single word being spoken, he knew she was deeply interested in him and for some reason that gave him an immense feeling of satisfaction. The interest was mutual, but before he pursued the beautiful Miss Bingley, or any woman for that matter, he needed to spend time in prayer. His responsibilities as a man of the cloth meant his partner in life had to share the same passion and he would not move forward unless God gave him peace about it.

"There are times I hate coming to Town." Max settled in the chair next to him. "Tonight, is no exception. It was bad enough when I was the heir apparent, but now that I have the title, complete strangers think they can toady up and be my best friend."

"I see Mrs. Hurst made an impression."

"How is it possible to set one's teeth on edge over a simple greeting? Thank goodness I never have to see them again."

"I hate to break this to you, but they are close friends of one Fitzwilliam Darcy. Also, their brother Charles stands alongside the master of Pemberley in a joint wedding ceremony. As one of the invited guests, you shall have to dance attendance to them for at least a week."

He almost laughed out loud at the look of chagrin which chased across Max's face.

"Dash it all! I was looking forward to his wedding." Max slumped back in his chair. Realizing others would notice his lack of decorum in such a public venue, he straightened and sat more erect. "Even in the semi dark, I can tell you are gaining much amusement from this."

"Oh yes, I am indeed. I shall be busy with my parish, but you will have to converse with them, eat every meal with them—"

"You have made your point, little brother," Max ground out between clenched teeth. "Of course, you are a perfect excuse to be absent for much of the festivities, and —" he held up a hand when Nathan attempted to interrupt "— you will gladly allow me to visit, every day if needed."

"You are always welcome, Max. You do not need to use me as an excuse."

"Are you sure you would not rather attend me at Pemberley?" Nathan wasn't fooled by the dulcet tone his brother used. He was up to mischief, much like the old days. "Miss Bingley certainly had eyes only for you, which given the circumstances is surprising. Should I be offended? I am the better catch, even though I did not kiss the fair maiden's hand."

"She certainly is beautiful." He let the last comment slide and glanced once more to the Marquis' box. Miss Bingley was being most attentive to her sister and seemed not to notice him looking her way. "I do not know if I'll call upon her."

"If I know you, Nathan, you will spend much time in prayer before chasing any woman. You have become a changed man and your priorities are different than a few years ago. This is not a decision you will make lightly and there is nothing wrong with that."

Nathan turned his attention away from the alluring Miss Bingley to his brother.

If it hadn't been for Max, he may never have changed his life around. After resigning his commission, he'd turned to gaming, drink and women in an effort to forget the atrocities of war and his reputation as a Rake became firmly established.

After many months, Max finally dragged him out of White's and confronted him. Broken and dissolute he'd confessed his sins and made the decision to join the church and attend seminary. Never would he forget his brother's actions, or how he listened as Nathan purged his soul of all he'd witnessed and done in France.

"If I am a changed man, it is because of you, Max," Nathan said quietly.

"I may have led you back to a relationship with God, but

He is the one who changed your heart." Max clapped him on the shoulder and then switched his attention back to the stage. "Now be quiet. The play is about to start. You can be maudlin tomorrow."

"I have no time to be maudlin. Between appointments with the Archbishop and our solicitor, I am to meet with the brides to ensure the Church of England they are prepared for the holy estate of marriage."

"Ugh, you sound like Father's old vicar. Please do not turn into a Mr. Power. He was a dreadful bore and absolutely no fun when invited over for Christmas punch."

"He did have a sour countenance. Well, I have no intentions of being like the dour Mr. Power." Both brothers chuckled at their childhood nickname for the somewhat resolute vicar. Nathan turned in his seat to face the stage. "Now, you be quiet. I want to enjoy the play."

"Lord Little Brat." Max teased, using his childhood nickname for Nathan.

"Lord Pompous Head." Nathan returned with a smile as the first actor took to the stage below.

Chapter Five

"Has the mail arrived?" Caroline asked Hobson almost as soon as she entered the house.

"No, Miss." Hobson slid the ermine lined redingote from her slim shoulders.

"Any callers while I was out." She kept the question casual but secretly held her breath while she removed her gloves and handed them over as well.

"No, Miss."

Disappointment flooded her heart. After gallantly bowing over her hand, she'd been positive Lord Nathan would follow up with a courtesy call, or at the very least, flowers. The past two days had seen nothing from the blasted man, which irritated her greatly. The banked heat in his eyes left her in no doubt of his attraction and she prepared for his anticipated visit by wearing a becoming dress both days. Today, she'd reluctantly took tea with Miss Grantley, and then chafed the whole time, worrying he'd come and gone.

It was ridiculous. One part of her hoped she hadn't missed him while the other part remained keenly frustrated there was no calling card on the silver tray to announce he'd even darkened their doorway. Louisa may have advised to cast her net on the other side of the boat, but what if the waters were bereft of anything to catch?

She moved into the music room and settled down at the pianoforte. Music was the only thing that calmed her soul these days and soon the melancholy sound of Mozart filled the air. Her mind continued down its tortuous path and the music rose and fell with each crescendo of thought.

Louisa cautioned against making his acquaintance as he was known about Town as a notorious Rake. He'd had his suit rejected by a young debutante a few years ago, although she did not know all the details. Her sister relied on second and third hand gossip concerning the higher levels of Society and Lord Nathan wasn't spoken of that much anymore. Apparently, he hadn't been in Town for a number of years.

About the eldest brother she seemed to be a veritable fount of information. He'd come into the title late last year and as a single man of only eight and twenty, with the title of Duke preceding his name, he could pick and choose any young lady to be wife.

Many of Society's mothers hoped to secure the young Duke's affection for their daughters. Caroline knew there was no hope of her coming into his stratosphere of influence, but his brother, the third in line shouldn't have too many strictures on whom he married. Her family may not be landed gentry, at least not until Charles finalized the purchase of Netherfield, and their money from trade was quite fresh, but she'd been sent to one of the most exclusive seminaries for young ladies in all of England and could hold her own with those of a higher pedigree. Too bad she had to attend her brother's dreadful wedding. Efforts to discover more about Lord Nathan would have to wait until she returned to Town.

Her fingers stilled on the keyboard, disquieting thoughts rendering her unable to continue playing. She was adrift and for the first time in three years had no set direction. Until Lord Nathan called upon her, if he called at all, she remained in limbo. There were no suitable men to dance attendance on her as the Season was winding down and at one and twenty she may as well be on the shelf.

She bitterly regretted refusing the young men who'd called upon her during her first Season in Town and mid-way through her second season their mother passed, forcing the whole family into a year of mourning. Regardless, it would not have mattered. Her focus had been solely on one Mr. Fitzwilliam Darcy of Pemberley, and look where that had gotten her.

Alone in a music room with nothing but Mozart to console her.

She gazed around the room. The only sound heard was the quiet bustle of servants going about their business. Not one soul cared whether she was there or not. She could collapse on the floor and expire and no one would be any wiser. When maids came to dust the room, only then would they discover her cold remains. She had no close friends to confide her hopes and fears with.

And whose fault would that be, my sweet Caroline, her grandmamma would ask as she rocked her recalcitrant granddaughter, soothing tears inevitably shed when Louisa or Charles would not include her in their activities. The answer was always, 'Mine'. How she missed her grandmamma with her soft voice and warm hugs.

She'd never been close to Louisa, six years her elder and Charles had been sent off to Eton and then Oxford, only coming home on special occasions, like Christmas. It wasn't until she came to London three years ago that she'd spent longer than a few weeks with either of them. With her father and mother both gone, the family home sold, she had no place to call her own.

And now with Charles marrying, she did not even have the luxury of looking after his household. Jane would rightfully become mistress of Netherfield Park. Unless she found a husband, she'd become the spinster aunt, relying on the good nature of family to place a roof over her head. Her lonely future stretched before her like an aching void.

She banged the keys in frustration. Why did Darcy have to fall in love with her?

"Are you playing one of the great Masters in the key of anger, Caroline?"

"Charles!" She gave a small start and placed a hand over her rapidly beating heart. "You must stop sneaking up on me at inopportune times."

He entered the room and stood beside the pianoforte.

"At least this time you have not ripped a pillow apart or fallen to the floor in tears. Things are improving."

"Do not remind me of that day. It is very ungallant of you to bring up how distraught I was."

"I came to ask if you would like to attend the Gardiner's with me. Jane and Miss Elizabeth have arrived for their trousseau fittings, as well as to meet with Darcy's vicar. I know they would love to see you while in Town."

Caroline raised an elegant brow at his last comment. Jane may have expressed those sentiments, but it would be a cold day in Hades before Eliza Bennet wished to see her. However, she'd promised to mend the rift between her and Charles.

Although the two Bennet sisters had, without malicious intentions, ruined the happiness she'd sought for three years, she needed to show them and the rest of society she bore no grudges. At the very least, make everyone believe she bore them no ill will.

"I would love to attend with you to Gracechurch Street. Such a quaint part of London, I remember it well when I last visited Jane."

At once she realized her faux pas when Charles became very still. For a moment she worried he'd refuse her company. He released a heartfelt sigh.

"I *am* disappointed in the way you sought to keep us separated, but this is a time of great joy for me and Jane and I refuse to harbor any anger. I hold you very dear, Caro. You are my baby sister and I will love you always."

Tears sprang to her eyes. To hear that her brother forgave and loved her was a soothing balm to her heart. She stood and hugged him tight. Until he'd said the actual words, she'd worried he would close his heart and life to her forever.

"And I love you, Charles." She stepped out of their familial embrace and he surprised her by offering a fresh linen cloth. She dabbed the corner of her eyes, which had gone quite moist with her emotional outburst. "You are forever supplying me with dry cloths."

"That is who I will be if needed, Steward of the Linen

Cupboard," he teased. "Now, move your body in the general direction of the front door. I am leaving in ten minutes."

"Are we not waiting for Louisa?"

"I spoke with her briefly. She is indisposed again and has taken to her bed. Let us be off."

"Please allow me to freshen up first."

"Ten minutes, Caroline. I will not wait a second longer," he threatened in a teasing voce and brought out his pocket watch, tapping the face of it.

She hurried from the room. There was one thing she wished give to Jane. An heirloom that had been passed down to Bingley brides for generations and would satisfy the 'something borrowed' part of the traditional, *Something old, Something new, Something borrowed, Something blue*.

An hour later saw Caroline seated in the front parlor of the Gardiner's residence on Gracechurch Street. Her memory of the room had been it was much too small to entertain guests, and the miniscule salon hadn't improved with two more bodies added to the venue. It also did not help her temperament that she was seated directly across from Miss Elizabeth Bennet and her Aunt Gardiner, whom she recognized from Pemberley. Miss Bennet and Charles were on the settee opposite and Mr. Gardiner reclined by the crackling fireplace, a mug of hot cocoa in his hand.

The first thing she'd noticed was how the usually reticent Jane Bennet bubbled with enthusiasm over the warehouses they would be attending. Secure in the affections of Charles, her personality shone through and Caroline had to admit that Jane truly loved her brother. It may have not been the match she and her sister, Louisa, desired, but his home would be a happy one and she felt an honest joy at the thought of their life together. A residual sliver of smugness crept into her heart at the thought of the annoying Mrs. Bennet being an inconvenient three miles from Netherfield Park. Thankfully, that was Charles' cross to bear.

Charles appeared to be all affability and easy charm, but if needed he would not hesitate to lay down a set of rules Mrs. Bennet may choose not to adhere. If so, she'd suffer stiff consequences. Such had been the case when they'd left their mother up North, in the family home.

One too many times mama sought to engage Charles' affections with daughters of friends and acquaintances. On his last visit from Oxford, she had the temerity to suggest he compromise a young lady in order to gain a substantial holding.

Horrified their mother might attempt something similar with his baby sister, barely ten and seven at the time, he'd whisked her off to London and plunked her down on Grosvenor Street with a newly married Louisa. The timing was such, mother could not argue as it allowed Caroline to have a Season as a debutante alongside her fellow classmates from Mrs. Rombough's School for Elegant Ladies.

"Your mother did not attend London with you?" Caroline asked of Jane.

"Mama is joining us near the end of the week." Jane slid a glance toward her sister, who joined in the conversation.

"Papa said Aunt Gardiner had enough on her plate with the two of us and her four children." Eliza's eyes sparkled with untold mischief. "She did not need to dance attendance on our mother as well. Mama was quite put out."

Caroline had a strong suspicion Mrs. Bennet would never stay within a budget and as such was not allowed to join.

"How long are you in Town? Do you have any further plans before returning to Longbourn?" Caroline asked the two sisters.

"We meet with Mr. Darcy's vicar tomorrow and the rest of our week is strictly for trousseau fittings." Miss Eliza answered. "Our days will be quite full with no time for entertaining anyone other than family."

"How kind then, that I was allowed to attend with Charles."

"Come now, Miss Bingley, Caroline, we are almost sisters. You are counted as family," Eliza rejoined. "In the future, I hope we shall always be of one mind, much like my dear Jane and I."

Although she smiled at Eliza and gave her a courteous nod at the seemingly kind words, Caroline caught an undercurrent of disdain. It had been no secret that she and the younger Miss Bennet did not enjoy each other's company and until today it never occurred to her that Miss Eliza Bennet held her in mild contempt.

Her conversation and manners, on the surface were of the utmost civility, but it was becoming more evident that Eliza Bennet found humor in her visit with Charles this afternoon. Why had she not seen the intelligence in this woman before? Plainly Darcy had, as he would never have given his affection to someone who could not hold his interest, or was only concerned with clothing and the latest hair styles. No, there was something more to Miss Bennet's character and although she did not want to admit it, not yet at least, she now understood something Darcy stated last time they were at Pemberley. He'd said that for many months he considered Elizabeth Bennet to be one of the handsomest women of his acquaintance.

At the time she'd been livid and refused to acknowledge that in a circular fashion he'd informed her that she, Caroline Bingley, was not handsome and he did not mean in physical beauty alone. But now, armed with an understanding of his decision, she knew he clearly meant body, heart and soul. The realization had a disquieting effect on her composure. Miss Elizabeth was forcing her to gaze upon a mirror where she did not approve of the reflected image.

Although unsettled by her observations, she'd come with intent to heal the breach, not to indulge in self-recrimination. She reached for her reticule.

"Seeing as Jane is about to become part of our family, I brought something for her to wear on her wedding day."

Jane cast a look of trepidation toward Elizabeth and for a brief moment Caroline regretted bringing the family heirloom. Did they think she was such a blackguard that she would give Jane something horrid? Eliza shook her head with the smallest of movement and Jane's shoulders relaxed.

Caroline almost stood and demand her brother take her home, not caring if he wasn't ready to leave. How dare they assume she... Remembrances of past conversations flitted through her memory. The Bennet sisters had every right to think she would say or do something horrid, and the fault lay solely on her shoulders. They had been the unhappy recipients of her unguarded tongue too many times in the past for her to expect reconciliation after one paltry note.

By this time, Charles had come to her side, a happy smile on his face. He'd probably guessed what she'd brought and knew she'd done the right thing.

"This was our great grandmother's and has been worn by every Bingley bride for over four generations. You may borrow it for your vows and pass it on to your own son's wife."

From her reticule she pulled out a jeweler's box which held the comb and handed it to Jane, who opened the box and gasped. Encrusted with tiny seed pearls and diamonds, the comb was meant to hold the bride's veil in place. Jane raised tear filled eyes to meet hers.

"Thank you, Caroline. I have no words to express my gratitude."

Against her will, Caroline's eyes became rimmed with tears as well. Whatever must the Miss Bennet's think of her?

Charles handed her and Jane fresh linen cloths. With a wry grin he looked at Caroline and stated, "The Steward of the Linen Cupboard at your service."

She smiled weakly at his humor. His attempt to apply levity to the situation was greatly appreciated.

Jane carefully placed the comb back into the jeweler's box and before closing the lid, gently ran her fingers over the beads and diamonds. Eliza, her fine eyes twinkling, watched Caroline dab the corner of her eyes with the cloth. For a few minutes she said not a word, only observed as both women composed themselves.

"You surprise me, Miss... Caroline." Elizabeth set down her tea cup and continued her inspection most intently.

"How is that?"

"You have brought my sister to tears of joy and humbled

yourself in sharing this moment without reservation. I would never have thought you capable of such honest emotion."

Her first instinct was to answer back in a scathing tone and show Miss Eliza Bennet what honest emotion really looked like. With great effort, she counted to ten before replying.

"As I checked the comb prior to attending your aunt's home, I had time to consider what may have gone through my great-grandmother's mind when she'd fastened it to her veil on her wedding day. And then again, what hopes and dreams did each Bingley bride up to my mother entertain?"

She glanced at Jane, still holding the box and smiling at something her brother said. What dreams did Jane have for her life with Charles? She felt as though her grandmamma was with her at that very moment, encouraging her to lay aside her hurt pride and extend an olive branch of friendship instead.

"Today is not about me, my dear sister Elizabeth, but about Jane and Charles. I truly hope they have a long and prosperous life together."

She'd have to be dead not to enjoy the flicker of surprise in Elizabeth's eyes at her remark. Before Elizabeth could continue the conversation, Charles came to stand beside them.

"It is time for us to take our leave, Caroline. It was lovely to see you again, Miss Elizabeth."

"Come, come, Mr. Bingley. We are to be brother and sister. As I have said to Caroline, you must call me by my Christian name. Family gatherings would be so tedious if we were forever calling each other Mr. or Miss."

"Quite right, Elizabeth. And I give you leave to call me Charles."

"Thank you, Charles," she said with a polite nod of her

head. "I presume we will not see you until we all arrive en masse at Pemberley?"

"Caroline and I arrive Friday prior to the week of the ball. Darcy and I want to get some shooting in. Louisa and Robert, Mr. Hurst, are traveling up with us."

"Splendid. I am looking forward to the ball, although my nerves are stretched a little tight at the thought of meeting Mr. Darcy's extended family."

And they of meeting yours, I would presume.

Caroline did not give voice to her malicious thoughts; instead she placed her tea cup on the small side table and stood.

"I informed Cook we would be home in time for dinner and I do not want her to hold the meal for us."

"Yes, yes. We should go." He gave Elizabeth a courteous bow and extended his arm for Caroline to place her hand upon.

She turned to Mrs. Gardiner. "Thank you for tea, Mrs. Gardiner. Mr. Gardiner."

Everybody said their polite goodbyes and Charles escorted her to the front door. When Jane joined them, Caroline took an inordinate amount of time pulling on her gloves to give them a moment of privacy. In less than two more weeks all this would be over and she could start again.

Chapter Six

Nathan scratched a few words on the paper before him, checking his Bible to assure himself he'd quoted the Scripture correctly.

"Is this where one comes to save his soul from eternal damnation?"

Nathan glanced up from his sermon making, a joyous smile creasing his face at the sound of a familiar voice.

"Maxwell!" He rose to his feet, skirted around the desk and clasped his eldest brother's outstretched hand. Before he could utter another word, his brother pulled him in for a hard hug. With enthusiasm, he returned the heart felt gesture. Although only a couple of weeks had passed since he last saw his brother, it felt like ages past. "What brings you to Derbyshire so early?"

"My affairs in London concluded sooner than expected, and Darcy invited me to shoot with him and other guests. As you know, I am not one for the social rounds and this came as a welcome reprieve." His brother stepped away and sat in the chair placed next to the crackling fireplace, comfortably crossing one leg over his knee. Nathan pulled the cord to ring his housekeeper for tea and then sat across from Max. "When we last met in London, you did not tell me you are to preside over the ceremony."

"Although it is his due, given his family connections, Darcy did not want the officiousness that comes with the Archbishop blessing his union. It would entail the whole wedding party to attend London and he greatly desired to get married at Pemberley. I gladly accepted the honor."

"You will officiate most admirably. I am curious about the woman who managed to bring our proud Mr. Darcy to one knee. Have you met Miss Bennet?"

"I have. Such a delightful young woman. Most amiable, full of extreme wit and charm."

The housekeeper appeared at the door. "Ye were wantin' something, Lord Reverend Kerr?"

"Yes, Mrs. Crenshaw. Could my brother and I have a spot of tea and some of your mouth-watering biscuits?"

"Right away, Lord Reverend Kerr sir, Your Grace." With much bobbing of her head she backed out of the room and disappeared down the hall toward the kitchen.

"That is quite the title you have there, brother," Max said with a smile.

"I know," Nathan sighed out. "I have asked her to simply call me Mr. Kerr, and we had some success. I think today she is a little discomposed over having a Duke in the parsonage. We will start again tomorrow."

He noted his brother's intent perusal.

"What? Have I got a blotch of ink on my shirt again?" He glanced down, moving his outer coat aside to inspect his chest.

Mrs. Crenshaw was forever scolding him about the amount of ink that *did not* make it onto the paper and implored him on a regular basis to wear only dark shirts when sermon writing.

"No," Max said carefully. "I have come to the realization you are quite content, here in Kympton, away from the hustle and bustle of London."

"I am." Nathan leaned forward. "I know Mother worried I would crawl into a northern corner of England, never to surface again after Miss Tottingham's refusal—"

"She was a fool," Maxwell interrupted with an indignant huff.

"Be that as it may, she was unwilling to move from London to Derbyshire and leave her family behind."

He waited for the familiar ache to rumble across his chest at the thought of Miss Tottingham, with her golden curls and liquid brown eyes, but nothing happened. His spirits lifted at the realization he could think of her without sorrow, or a feeling of loss.

"She wanted a titled family and elegant parties in London, Nathan. Do not try to make her into a saint when she was not."

Max stopped speaking when Mrs. Crenshaw arrived with a tray. They both waited while she poured them a cup of tea, and with a curtsy and more bobbing of the head, left the room.

"We will not speak of Miss Tottingham again. She is in the past and shall stay there. When and if the Lord sees fit to bring me a wife, she will be someone who has a heart for the downcast and doesn't mind mending her own stockings."

"Then do not set your cap for any of Darcy's guests," Max said with a laugh. "Most of his family are Lord this and Lady that. There will be so much blue blood in attendance the King himself might think it's a royal coronation and show up."

Both brothers laughed and then settled in to discuss family happenings and enjoy their tea. After catching up on what their mother was keeping busy with and how George was breaking many hearts in London, Nathan pressed deeper.

"Is there any young lady who has captured your interest this Season, brother?"

"Not you too." Max set his cup onto the table with a bang. Immediately he grimaced. "Sorry, old chap. I do not mean to break your tea service, but that question has dogged me for over two years and I am dashed tired of it. It was annoying when I was just the heir, but now that I have got the title, the sharks have my scent in the water."

"You will be nine and twenty on your next birthday, and if you wish to marry and have children at an age where you can actually enjoy them..." He trailed off and waited in silence.

"There is one—"

"Ha! I knew it. I knew there was someone. My left eyebrow twitches whenever you have a secret."

"That is an old wives' tale and I am surprised you even adhere to that hobble-dee-hoy." Max flicked an imaginary speck of dust from his leg, a frown marring his elegant brow.

"Protest if you must, but I knew there was something. Your letters have been most melancholy and we did not have time to really discuss anything of import when I was last in London."

"She is not ready for marriage."

"Please tell me she is at least out of the nursery."

"Yes, she is." Max practically glowered at Nathan.

"Does she view you in the same light?"

"I do not know." Max sighed deeply. "I love her without question, but she has not really experienced anything beyond her home."

"As your brother I wish you to find contentment. As a minister with the Church of England, I would advise you to continue to exercise caution. Once married, it is until death do you part. Do not make the same mistake our uncle made with the hoyden he tied his anchor to."

"Ah, yes, Uncle Moreland. He did grab a tiger by the tail with Millicent, more than twenty years his junior." Max stroked his chin as he continued in remembrance. "Who knew someone who sang like an angel with the most innocent of expressions would have no less than three lovers on the go?"

"It was not three, Max. There was only one and that was enough to ruin their good names."

Nathan rang the bell for Mrs. Crenshaw to clear away the tea service. "This is your first time here. Would you care to see the rest of the house and garden?"

"I would. This is an extremely good living Darcy had available. The house is quite large."

Both men stood and walked toward the front foyer. Nathan started the tour by pointing out the generous music room with an attached library.

"The library is nothing compared to our ancestral home or that of Pemberley, but there are enough tomes here to keep me entertained for a few years. Come this way to the dining room."

The tour did not take too long. The vicarage boasted a dining room large enough to entertain twelve guests comfortably and the kitchen had a well-stocked larder. In the back, Mrs. Crenshaw had a garden as well as a hot house for growing food during the winter months. Upstairs, there were eight bedrooms, four of which had attached bathing chambers. The third level had enough rooms for at least five servants, but as Nathan was a single man, he only needed two.

At the end of the tour Nathan escorted his brother down to the stables. There he housed three horses, two that Darcy provided for his modest carriage and his own stallion, Thunder, for riding. He found he needed his trusty steed to travel about the estate looking after his parishioners while keeping the carriage for more formal affairs or inclement weather.

"I am pleased for you, Nathan and will assure Mother you have landed on your feet, and are content with life after serving in the military for so long."

Nathan's stable master brought Max's horse over to where they stood.

"Thank you, Peter."

Peter touched the brim of his hat and turned back toward the stable. Nathan noted the horse had only a saddle.

"Did you not bring a change of clothes?"

"I had my valet go on ahead with the carriage," Max chuckled. "I was anxious to see you again. This upcoming week will be busy for both of us."

Nathan clasped his brother's outstretched hand. "I wish you would stay here, but I understand that Mr. Darcy wants all the guests to partake in activities at the main house."

"True, plus the ball this coming Thursday. It is so much easier to find one's bed when it is in the same house."

"The ball. I had forgotten."

"You are invited?"

"Of course. I may be his vicar, but I am also Lord Nathan. Mr. Darcy was most insistent I attend. Who am I to say 'no' at the chance to see old friends and acquaintances?"

"And the beautiful Miss Bingley again."

"She is beautiful, there is no argument there, however, I have some concerns to her character."

"How is that? You had no great discussion with her."

"I have not had any amount of conversation with her, but when I conducted my interview with the Bennet sisters last week, some things arose that gave me pause."

"I would not listen to idle gossip, brother. Make your own decisions."

"Do not misunderstand. The Bennet sisters were charming and are the souls of discretion. When we spoke of Charles Bingley's family, they demurred when discussing Miss Bingley. It was not what they said, but what they did not say."

He stepped back as Max mounted his large bay horse.

"Nathan, you have never judged someone by the opinions of others. Their view is skewered by their own prejudices. Give the lady a chance to prove herself. You may be pleasantly surprised."

"You are right as always, but it would be a shame if such a lovely package held nothing good inside."

The stallion sidestepped and huffed, anxious to be off.

"I must go before Pericles misbehaves and attempts to unseat me. I shall see you tonight at Pemberley."

"Tonight?"

"I forgot to tell you. We have been invited by Darcy to dine there this evening." Max dug his heels into the sides of the stallion and took off at a fast pace. "Until tonight," he called over his shoulder.

Nathan waved a salute goodbye and stood at the end of his walk until his eldest brother was out of sight. A smile creased his face at the thought of seeing the lovely Caroline Bingley at Pemberley this evening. Already he looked forward to speaking with her further and determine for himself what type of woman she truly was.

~~~ooo0ooo~~~

Caroline, Louise, Mr. Hurst, Charles and Darcy gathered in the drawing room and listened to Georgiana play the small pianoforte. The ladies commandeered the scattered couches, while the men stood near the fireplace. Darcy had informed them two more guests were expected and once they arrived they'd proceed to the dining room.

"Who do you think the other guests are?" Louisa whispered, apparently not noticing the annoyed look Darcy shot toward them. Caroline did not blame him. Georgiana was such a talented pianist and she executed the intricate piece written by Beethoven like a master. She could listen to the young girl play all night, but Louisa kept interrupting with hushed murmurs and caustic observations. As of late, her sister's mien fluctuated between joy and happiness to behaving in a taciturn and petulant manner, all within the blink of an eye. Caroline never knew which woman would walk through the door. About to chastise her sister for being rude, the door to the drawing room opened and Grieves opened the double doors, admitting the Duke of Adborough and his brother, Nathan.

Lord Nathan was here! Her heart beat a rapid tattoo and her breath came in quick, short bursts. Never in her dreams had she thought to see him at Pemberley of all places. After many days of no calling cards or visits she assumed he was still a Rake and their light flirtation, although exciting, meant nothing to him. Clearly, they were here for the wedding. She'd wondered how far Darcy's reach was into the Peerage, but never once thought of a Duke.

Quickly and without a lot of fanfare, Darcy introduced the Duke to Charles. For some odd reason he did not introduce Lord Nathan and Charles behaved as though they were already acquainted. She found it interesting, yet quite confusing. When Darcy turned to reference the Hurst's and Caroline, the Duke nodded at them politely.

"Good evening."

Caroline did not miss the frosty tone His Grace used. He did not even tell Darcy they'd been introduced prior to this evening. Louisa had not made a favorable impression that evening at the theatre, but there wasn't much she could do about that now. As grandmamma would say – that horse left the barn already.

"Shall we proceed to the dining room? My cook, Mrs. Pike has outdone herself today."

"If I remember correctly," the Duke teased in a familiar way. "I tried to entice your cook away from you. I am most envious, Darcy."

The Duke's reference to members of Darcy's household made Caroline realize how familiar they were with one another. Another clue was the ease with which Darcy behaved around the two titled brothers, a gentle reminder of his noble heritage.

"I am very humbled by the fidelity my staff bestow me on

a daily basis. Most of them have been at Pemberley since I was a child. I would become bereft if any of them left."

"That is true. Your Mrs. Reynolds is a treasure. She keeps this house moving like a well-oiled carriage."

Caroline gave a start at the mention of Mrs. Reynolds, the woman she'd have replaced without one thought or remorse. How blind she'd been to so many things with regard to Darcy, Georgiana and Pemberley and the reminder of her arrogance settled about her shoulders like an itchy shawl.

There wasn't much time to ponder these truths as they proceeded to the dining room without further delay. Darcy took his place at the head of the table, with the Duke on his right, Georgiana on his left with Charles and then Louisa seated next. Much to Caroline's consternation she was seated between Mr. Hurst and Lord Nathan. Beneath the table she fidgeted with her gloves, not knowing what to say or do. The last time she'd been in Lord Nathan's company, he'd held her hand, given her a most intense look and spent an inordinate amount of time watching her at the opera. At least that was her impression as every time she'd sent a covert glance in his direction, he'd been watching their box.

"You are a long way from London, Miss Bingley."

Lost in her thoughts, she gave a small start when Lord Nathan addressed her.

"As are you, Lord Nathan."

To calm her nerves, she removed her gloves and laid them across her lap. Mr. Hurst picked up his linen napkin and tucked it into his cravat. Oh dear, she'd forgotten what a messy eater he could be and hoped none of his dinner would spatter its way onto her new dress.

"Do you have any hobbies, Miss Bingley?"

"I play the pianoforte and stitch embroidery."

"How industrious."

She snapped her attention to him more closely. Although his countenance was serene, she caught a glint of mischief in his surprisingly grey eyes. She picked up her napkin and settled it on her lap, ever mindful to make sure a majority of the cloth covered her skirt nearest to Mr. Hurst.

"And what other activities do you pursue in your spare time?" His questions continued.

"Well, I... There is much to do in Town." She cast about trying frantically to think of what she did to fill her spare time. "I visit with friends and shop—"

"All very interesting and London is diverting, but what do you *do*?"

"Do?"

"Yes. *Do*. Such as visit the infirm, or take baskets of food to those in need. What do you do?"

Flummoxed, she sat in total silence for what felt like forever. Whatever did she do with her time? Surely, she could come up with one good deed and when was that footman going to bring her soup?

"I spend a lot of time writing correspondence. I have a great many friends I stay in touch with from my school years."

She stopped herself from crossing her fingers at the outright lie. If truth be told, she rarely wrote because there were few friends to correspond with. She had a beautiful escritoire with a stack of personalized stationery and a pot full of ink. In contrast, when Elizabeth Bennet stayed at Netherfield to care for her sister, she'd written four letters that she knew of, maybe more in those few short days.

Never before had she realized how empty her life had become.

"Did you enjoy the remainder of the play, Miss Bingley?"

"Yes, very much." She grasped at the new conversational straw Lord Nathan provided. "And you?"

"The play was acceptable, but I found my attention diverted."

At his flirtatious tone, her tongue almost cleaved to the top of mouth, it went so dry.

"I am not sure what would have diverted your attention, Lord Nathan. I found the play riveting." She took a small sip of water to moisten that pesky dry as Sahara mouth.

"Then you must have found humor in Bertrand's entrance."

"Bertrand?"

She tried in vain to remember to whom he referred. The knowing smile Lord Nathan bestowed on her caused her stomach do a traitorous flip.

"Bertrand was the main character and as he declared his love to Rosamund, he tripped on a cushion and fell into her lap."

Surely, he jested. No such thing happened, but then again, she'd spent the better part of the play casting furtive glances toward his private box, only to find his gaze fixed firmly on her. It was one of the main reasons she'd been assured he would place a social call in the days following.

"My apologies to the talented actors on stage. I must admit my attention was diverted to the wellbeing of my sister as she has not been feeling well of late." She paused as a footman finally placed a bowl of soup in front of her. Once the footman was out of ear-shot, Lord Nathan resumed their conversation.

"Are you pleased with your brother's upcoming nuptials?"

"I am. Charles is so very happy."

"And you? Do you support his choice of bride?"

She paused, her brow furrowing. For someone not directly involved with their family, Lord Nathan showed uncommon concern about whom Charles married. Did he not approve of Charles marrying someone of such low consequence and by proxy, disapprove of Darcy's choice as well? There was a time she'd have danced with glee that someone of nobility and rank saw the disparity between the two families, but that was before her eyes were opened as to why Charles and Darcy released their hearts to the Bennet sisters.

Although she may have not been happy with Charles' choice at first, she'd come to the realization Jane made her brother exquisitely happy and he, her. It really was no one else's business who arrived at the altar beside him.

"Miss Jane Bennet is a lovely girl and I am proud to call her sister." The minute she said the words, she knew without a doubt she meant them. "She is uncommonly genteel and Charles is ecstatic at the thought of their future lives together."

She cut off further attempts at conversation by picking up her spoon and eating. She could not be certain, but she thought she heard him murmur, '*Well done*'.

Chapter Seven

"I say Darcy, I just found out your vicar is the brother of His Grace, the Duke of Adborough."

"Yes, he is."

Charles and Darcy were the last of the gentlemen to leave the dining room after enjoying a glass of port and some gentleman-like conversation. Or as Darcy's sister, Georgiana, liked to tease, '*What horse am I going to ride, buy or bet on*'. He appreciated his sister's capricious sense of humor, which had not been much in evidence of late, and dared not tell her she was very close to the truth in her assessment.

The Duke, his brother and Mr. Hurst had already gone on ahead to the drawing room when Charles pulled him aside with the knowledge of who Mr. Kerr truly was.

"That's all? You have nothing more to say? Why did you keep this from me?"

"I am sorry, Bingley. I should have told you. Given the propensity of our future mother-in-law to morph into a sycophant when in the presence of wealth or title, I determined to keep Mr. Kerr's familial relations quiet."

"Yes, yes. Quite." Charles nodded in understanding. "Still, you should have told me."

Darcy felt a momentary twinge of guilt. He'd made it an extremely bad habit of underestimating this young man. First, he'd kept Jane Bennet's visit to London a secret and very nearly ruined their chance and his for happiness, and now he'd dithered in making Charles aware of Mr. Kerr's austere connections. Elizabeth was right. He did have a tendency to project a selfish disdain toward others and he was not used to sharing all of his thoughts and opinions.

"I promise from now on I shall be as clear as a crystal ball with you. Nothing will be hidden. You are a man I trust implicitly and can only ask that you forgive me."

Charles acquiesced with a slight nod. "You know I cannot stay mad at you. Besides, Jane would never forgive me if I held a grudge. She finds the good in everybody, my sweet angel."

"I must give you one caution. Your sister, Caroline, has been known to... impress herself among those who will not appreciate her efforts." He gazed keenly into his young friend's eyes, trying to ascertain whether Charles caught his meaning. He'd spoken with him before of how he'd caught her sneaking between the guest and family wing on their last visit in August. Although nothing untoward happened, he'd made sure to lock his bedroom door after that. He had no desire to be trapped in a loveless marriage. If he wanted that, he'd have married his cousin, Anne.

"I know exactly what you mean. As you know, I tried to steer Caroline toward gentleman who would appreciate our background and close connection with trade. This discussion may be moot anyway."

"Why do you say that?"

"It seems my sisters have already been introduced to the Lord Kerr's in London."

"I find that hard to believe. What connection would they have with regard to them?"

"My brother-in-law, Mr. Hurst is an acquaintance of the Marquis of Dorchester," Charles sighed out. "He attended Cambridge with him. Mr. Hurst and my sisters were part of a larger party that attended the theatre where they were introduced to the Duke and his brother, Lord Nathan. According to Louisa, Lord Nathan flirted with Caroline."

Darcy stayed silent for a few minutes, processing what Charles revealed.

"Caroline has no knowledge Lord Nathan is my vicar?"

"From what Mr. Hurst told me this very evening, they have no knowledge of his position at all."

"Hmm…. This puts us in a very interesting position," Darcy finally stated, a hint of humor coloring his tone.

"How is that?"

"Elizabeth is always encouraging me to find levity in certain situations. I have a sudden desire to stay back and see how all this plays out between your sister and Lord Nathan."

"Darcy, that is somewhat cruel." Charles choked back a laugh. "However, I will stand with you and keep my peace. My sister has much to learn of human behavior and what, in life, should be held in esteem."

"However, we are in accord that Mrs. Bennet shall be kept unaware?"

"Oh yes. Very much in accord."

Both men shook hands then proceeded to the drawing

room where everyone awaited their arrival.

~~~ooo0ooo~~~

Caroline sat on a small couch; her fingers laced tightly together to keep from fidgeting. Ever since she was a child, when faced with turmoil, she'd pull threads, shred ribbons, anything to quell her anxiety. She did not need to pull all the lovely golden ribbons woven through her deep green dress.

The men were still enjoying their port after Louisa, Georgiana and herself repaired to the drawing room. She had to give much credit to Georgiana. As the only Darcy female in attendance, the burden of hostess fell upon her young shoulders. Although a bit too reticent to proclaim tonight's festivities a grand success, the young woman made sure everybody had tea and was engaged in conversation.

Under normal circumstances, the men would generally tarry anywhere from half an hour to an hour with their port, but tonight the door to the drawing room opened after only a quarter of an hour had chimed. She assumed Darcy hurried them along so his shy sister would not be left on her own for too long.

She braced herself for the appearance of the Duke, as he would take precedence in returning and knew his brother would immediately follow. With great will power she trained her line of sight beyond the annoying Lord Nathan, with expectation of seeing Darcy and then Charles, but only Mr. Hurst came through the door.

Her agitation grew to a fever pitch. From the corner of her eye she saw the gentleman who'd dominated her thoughts more than she liked began to move in her direction. Where was Charles? He was her anchor. Without his calming presence she felt as though she bobbed about the surface of the water and Lord Nathan a hurricane force wind about to descend.

"Miss Darcy," she called out in desperation. "Would you play something for us?"

When Georgiana consented with a graceful nod of her head, Caroline almost leapt to her feet and met her at the pianoforte. Clearly wondering why Caroline was suddenly being so attentive after years of neglectful condescension, Georgiana took her seat, brow furrowed. A pinch of conscience made Caroline ashamed of her past behavior and she smiled down at the young woman.

"Let me turn the pages for you." She stoically refused to look up and see where Lord Nathan had taken his imposing presence. "Then you do not have to worry about losing your place."

"Thank you, Miss Bingley."

With great determination, she kept her focus on Georgiana and her playing. Even so, it did not take long before the music transported her mind and calmed her heart. All too soon Georgiana finished the piece. She looked up at Caroline and gave her a shy smile.

"Would you play another piece. I could listen to you all night."

"Thank you, Miss Bingley." Miss Darcy's cheeks warmed and her smile held no guile. "I have played enough this evening. I would love to hear something from you."

Caroline noted Charles and Darcy come into the drawing room. Charles surged ahead of Darcy, exclaiming, "Yes, please do, Caro. I have not heard you play a full piece in ages."

She knew by the twinkle in his eye he referred to last week

where he'd caught her banging the keys in anger.

"It would be my pleasure. Do you have any requests?" Out of habit, she looked toward the fireplace where Darcy stood with the Duke. Odd how she still deferred to him, even when she knew he held no regard for her, if he ever had at all.

"Are you familiar with Mozart?" The dulcet tones of Lord Nathan made her stomach quiver. He was standing not more than three feet from her.

Without uttering a word, she nodded and took her seat.

"Do you require the sheet music, Miss Bingley?" Georgiana asked.

"No thank you, Miss Darcy. I will play a piece I am familiar with."

Lord Nathan escorted Georgiana back to her seat while she settled at the pianoforte, cleared her mind and began to play *Eine Klein Nachtmusik*. As her fingers flew over the keyboard, she heard the music exactly as she had the first time she attended a concert with her father in Edinburgh. In her mind violins and cellos kept perfect harmony, transporting the music to unheard of heights.

To think, Caro, Mozart t'was but a boy when he wrote this music. Can you believe he started writin' when he was a wee lad, three years of age? There's nothin' you cannot do if you set your mind to it.

Her father's rough northern accent held awe at what was achievable and she'd never forgotten that night. It changed her whole life and from that moment, music became her passion.

When she finished to polite applause and took a seat in a nearby chair, Louisa played and sang a popular piece. She did not have a strong voice, but it was enjoyable.

From her vantage point across the room, Caroline

watched Lord Nathan as he conversed with Georgiana. Head bent in conversation, broad shoulders turned slightly toward the young girl, he intrigued her, this man of mystery. He was exceedingly handsome, to be sure, but other than that she knew nothing about him. Not a whisper of where he'd been for the past three years.

Georgiana's eyes lit up and she smiled at something he said. Obviously, he was a kind soul, to spend time with Darcy's shy sister. Not many people, herself included, thought to include her in their conversations. They mostly spoke to her, not with her.

That nugget of understanding dropped heavy in her heart. All those times she'd enquired after the health of Darcy's sister, or of what endeavor she may be engaged with, she truly hadn't cared what his response would be. All of it had been a pitiful attempt to squeeze his attention back to her.

She recalled in August, when Elizabeth Bennet had come to Pemberley with her Aunt and Uncle, she'd spent much of the evening quietly conversing with Georgiana. In retrospect, Miss Bennet's behavior bordered on being protective, as though she'd been shielding Miss Darcy from her and her sister.

Sadly, she and Louisa had not once spoken with Georgiana. All they'd done was ridicule Miss Bennet and her family. Caroline looked down at her clasped hands, resting on her lap. Her grandmamma would have been so disappointed.

Georgiana's soft laugh brought her attention back to her and Lord Nathan. Caroline longed to have him give her the same undivided attention. Evidently sensing her study of him, he shifted his gaze toward her. Quickly she looked down, but almost against her will, she raised her eyes and found him watching her intently. She could not look away, although her mind and senses urged her to. As if he knew her thoughts, like words being displayed on parchment, his mouth quirked at one corner and he inclined his head.

Her face flamed and prickles of heat threatened to turn her cheeks an unbecoming pink. As a precautionary measure, she snapped open her fan. The gold pomander on her wrist swayed with each flick of her wrist, setting off a pleasant aroma of her favorite rose water. She allowed the familiar scent to soothe her. It would not do for Lord Nathan to know he discomposed her.

$$\sim\sim\sim ooo0ooo\sim\sim\sim$$

Nathan listened with half an ear as Miss Darcy chattered about the upcoming ball. In no way would he reveal to the delightful young woman that his attention was fully riveted on the lovely Miss Caroline Bingley. As usual she wore a gown that was both bold, yet understated. Her modiste, evidently a virtuoso with needle and thread, had pieced the emerald silk in such a way that the material, and the woman beneath, captured his interest.

He'd had full intention of conversing with her after enjoying some quiet time with the men. Those plans were for naught because when he entered the room, she'd rushed to join Miss Darcy at the pianoforte. As a former connoisseur of women, he understood her ploy to delay their interaction for what it truly was. She fought the attraction between them and seemed to be losing the battle.

He had to admit a strong surge of disappointment whereupon entering the room he noticed her attention focused on those who followed behind. Or more specifically, Mr.

Darcy. Obviously, Miss Bingley still held some sort of misguided affection for the Master of Pemberley, one that must fade away as Darcy would soon wed Miss Elizabeth.

His awareness of the red-haired beauty could no longer be denied; however, it would be in his best interest to proceed with caution. A liaison, even a closer friendship with her was fraught with danger. During their conversation at supper, he'd pressed to find out where her interests lay and like most ladies in Society and her time was indeed wasted by frivolous activities.

Yet when she'd played the pianoforte for this small gathering of family and friends, he knew he'd been given a glimpse of her soul. Through her passion, she transported them all to a place of beauty and that was a God given talent. One not to be taken lightly.

There was much depth to this spoiled miss and he'd be remiss if he did not discover what went on in the mind of Miss Caroline Bingley. He turned his gaze toward her, still seated beside the pianoforte and caught her watching him. Quickly, she averted her attention to her clasped hands and he willed to look at him again, which she did.

A purely masculine thrill rushed through him by the emotion laid bare upon her face. He gave her a knowing smile and inclined his head. He too felt the invisible threads that seemed to be knitting their lives together.

He spoke with Miss Darcy few more minutes and then excused himself and moved to the other side of the room, stopping before the couch where the lady who held his interest sat.

"I compliment you on your talent, Miss Bingley." He

watched closely to gauge her reaction. Would she be condescending, or gracious? Much would be gleaned on how she received praise. "Rarely have I heard Mozart played so passionately."

"Thank you, Lord Nathan." She toyed with the pomander on her wrist. "Your praise should be reserved for Mozart, who wrote such beautiful music. I am but a vessel for his genius."

Pleased with her answer, he decided on a bold move.

"May I join you?" He did not wait for an answer but pulled forward a small stool and sat beside the couch. "I hate when people have to crick their necks in order to speak with me."

"You are tall, Lord Nathan." She gathered her skirts and moved them away from the leg of the stool. "Forgive me. I know what it is like to have people comment on your height."

He paused at her statement. What she said was true. Miss Bingley was above average height, which did not bother him as he stood a good six inches over her, but to others within their acquaintance, she would appear to be an Amazonian goddess.

"Yes, I suppose you would. Like me, I am sure you were always asked to pick the apples others could not reach." She smiled and nodded. "And I would hazard a guess you have been asked many times, by caring family members only," he teased, "how the weather was up there." She now laughed softly. "Then I suggest, for the duration of these festivities, you and I stay close together whenever we are in each other's company. To lend each other moral support," he hastened to add when her cheeks tinged pink. His suggestion was outrageous, but he liked the thought of having her close by him.

"I do not quite know what to say, Lord Nathan." She carefully shifted on the couch to put more space between them.

"I believe you are teasing me."

In prior years, when he was a jaded man, he would have relentlessly pursued her. She stirred his blood like no woman had, not even Miss Tottingham, to whom he'd proposed marriage. At that moment Mrs. Hurst joined them.

"Lord Nathan. It is such a pleasure to see you again." Her smile stretched wide with no hint of warmth, or sincerity. "I did not have opportunity to speak with you over dinner."

"Such are the vagaries of life," he replied with a careless shrug.

Georgiana approached them. "Excuse me. My brother and I set up tables for a few games of cards. Would you care to join us and even out the numbers?"

"I love to play cards." Louisa hastened to her feet and settled at the card table near where Maxwell stood talking to Darcy. She was quickly joined by Charles, Mr. Hurst and Georgiana and he noted that she struggled to hide her disappointment. As the foursome for the one group had been decided, Nathan offered Miss Bingley his arm.

"Miss Bingley, may I escort you to our table?"

"Thank you, but I am capable of walking on my own," came her tart reply. She stood, shook out her skirts and proceeded to the other table with Nathan close behind. They were joined by his brother and Darcy.

He fully expected Caroline to preen and gloat at her good luck when she realized she'd be sitting with all the principal men of their company. Instead, she cast a quick glance at her sister, appearing more worried than prideful.

He could not help a small smile at the knowledge that if both sisters knew how bad Max was at cards, neither of them would wish to partner with him. Yet he wondered at the dynamics of their sisterly relationship. Surely Mrs. Hurst would want her sister to command the attention of not one, but two available men. Then again, he'd seen how she genuflected in the presence of his brother, so nothing should surprise him anymore.

He partnered with Darcy, with the intent to win and his brother graciously partnered with Miss Bingley. After a few quick hands, Nathan realized she was extremely intelligent and extremely skilled. It was as though she knew where each card was and who held them. If she were a man, he'd take her to White's and make a bag full of money. Under her guidance, she and Max dominated the set. When he'd pressed her at the dinner table about what she did with her time, wanting to know what made her tick, nothing prepared him for this particular ability.

Not only did she have skill as a card player, but between dazzling plays, she bantered with Darcy, and spoke to his brother with surprising candor. He knew Max found this refreshing as almost all of London held him in awe. And during all this, not once did she miss a move.

The only person she treated with extreme caution was him. There was a tug between them, an undercurrent beneath the calm civility of their conversations, much like the river close to his ancestral home. One false move and you'd be pulled beneath the seemingly placid water. For now, he and Miss Bingley were balancing rather tenuously on a flat bottom raft, neither willing to tip the balance for fear of that current.

Chapter Eight

The melancholy strains of *Ignaz Pleyel's* sonata in F Major flowed from Caroline's fingertips onto the pianoforte keyboard. She let the music take her away to a world of beauty and peace. At times like this, she forgot about her frustration of gaining not one toe hold in the impenetrable wall of society. She forgot the heartache threatening to consume her very being. She forgot who she was. A woman whose wealth came from not from titled lands and nobility, but from trade. The very type of people she besmirched every chance she had. People like her grandmamma, whose work roughened fingers wiped more than one tear away from her cheeks as she grew up.

The music came to an abrupt halt and Caroline hung her head in shame. If grandmamma were alive and knew what she'd become, how she behaved...it did not bear thinking about. Needless to say, her grandmother's heart would be broken. Cora Bingley raised her family to be proud of their heritage. Nothing wrong ever came from hard work, was a phrase oft repeated in the Bingley household.

With limited choices in the running, Louisa settled on Mr. Hurst whose family had a reasonable estate in Warwickshire, albeit smaller than what the Bennet's laid claim to at Longbourn. Not that they'd ever reveal that to anyone. Louisa achieved the status of a gentleman's wife in her marriage and her children would be accepted in places Caroline could only dream of.

That was when she became determined to attain a higher standing than a gentleman who brought in less than two thousand pounds per annum. She'd make a marriage worthy of her dowry and with that goal in mind, set her cap at Mr. Darcy, who never regarded her in the same light no matter how hard she tried. She'd seen his interest in Elizabeth Bennet at Netherfield when she arrived to nurse her sister back to health and no matter how hard she attempted to throw the country miss into an unfavorable light; he'd turned all incidents into praise worthy events. She should have known his heart was engaged right then. How arrogant she'd been, assuming he'd return to London and once out of Miss Bennet's illuminous sphere be drawn to her.

She stood and walked to the diamond paned window and stared out over the beautiful grounds without really seeing anything. Her life was adrift and last night, after she'd excused herself to go to bed, Louisa visited. Her pride, pricked over a perceived slight from the Duke, motivated her to harangue Caroline about her selfish behavior. She then advised she was with child and Caroline would have to find lodgings elsewhere as her suite would be turned into a nursery.

The clock chimed the eleventh hour and Caroline decided to go for a walk. Rambling about the grand house held no allure and for once, even her music could not soothe her restlessness. She had Lucy bring down a cashmere shawl for her shoulders. It was such a pleasant day there was no requirement for anything heavier.

"Do you wish me to accompany you, Miss?"

"No, Lucy. I shall stay close to the house. I only want some fresh air before dinner."

"Yes, Miss." Lucy curtsied and Caroline exited the great house via the morning room which opened to a wide expanse of manicured garden, the roof of the stable visible over a small berm just to the west.

The quiet nicker of horses drew her toward the stables and she entered the spacious building, anxious to see the horse Darcy spoke of the other night. He'd purchased a lovely mare for Elizabeth as a wedding present and she was curious as to what type of mount he'd chosen. Would she be a gentle creature, or something with more spirit? With some knowledge of Miss Bennet's character, she leaned toward Darcy choosing a more spirited animal.

There were at least twenty stalls and she checked the first two, finding them empty. About to exit the second stall, she heard Lord Nathan's deep voice. Botheration. She did not want to face him so soon after last night's dinner party. He was cheeky enough to misconstrue her intent and declare she followed him. She slipped back into the stall and listened to their muffled voices.

When all she heard was the gentle rhythm of horses in their stalls, she advanced and peeked down the main corridor of the stable. Her shoulders relaxed and she took a deep cleansing breath.

He hadn't seen her. Thank goodness.

$$\sim\sim\sim ooo0ooo\sim\sim\sim$$

Nathan entered the Pemberley stables, amazed at how spacious and airy the building was. Each stall had an arched entrance with a small portico before you entered the area where the horses were housed. Inside each portico, various brushes and farrier instruments hung in perfect order. Saddles and tack were suspended on strong hooks across the other side of the entranceway. He knew Max, after seeing the layout of the stable, would authorize changes at Adborough Hall. Of that he had no doubt.

Darcy exited one of the stalls near the middle and upon seeing him, approached with a firm stride.

"Kerr. Glad you could meet me here. I am a bit busy and this was the only time I could spare." He reached into his waistcoat and pulled out an envelope. "I was hoping you could incorporate these words into the marriage ceremony. It is meant to be a surprise for Elizabeth."

"Certainly." Nathan took the envelope and tucked it into his own pocket.

"Would you like to see my wedding gift for Elizabeth?" Darcy's voice was full of happiness and had a lightness Nathan never noticed before. He admired Miss Bennet for bringing out the softer side of Darcy and knew their marriage would be one full of love and encouragement.

He nodded his head in agreement and followed Darcy back into the stall he'd exited a few moments ago.

"She is a beauty, Mr. Darcy." Nathan ran his hands over the mare's shoulder and back.

"I have told you before, call me Darcy. I know I am your

patron, but we have known each other for years."

"Very well, but allow me to show you proper respect when others are around."

"We shall see, Kerr. I am not that much of a stickler for protocol with those I trust."

Surprise had Nathan pause for a moment. To be told by a man, whose reputation of being distant and proud was legendary, that he trusted him filled him with a sense of gratitude and friendship. The mare nickered and nudged his pocket for the apple she scented.

"May I?" he queried and after a quick nod from Darcy placed the apple on his palm. Within seconds the crisp fruit disappeared and she nudged his pocket for more. "Sorry, Athena. Next time I visit."

Both men turned to exit the stall.

"Do you think Elizabeth will like my wedding gift?"

"It depends. Does Miss Bennet ride?"

"She assured me she rides, but she's fonder of walking. In order to see all the estate, a horse makes more sense."

"I agree. Even a most ardent walker could not cover all the area in less than a month."

"I have—" Darcy stopped when the head groomsman approached. "Yes, Dobson?"

Sorry, Mr. Darcy, sir. There's been a spot of trouble with the new mare you bought for Miss Darcy. She's sounding a bit wheezy."

"Go ahead, Darcy. I can see myself out," Nathan stated.

"Very well, thank you."

Darcy and Dobson turned and made haste toward the other end of the stable. A short huffing sound had him stop and peer inside the next stall. Inside stood a large stallion, his coat gleamed ebony black and his eyes had a proud look about them.

"You are a handsome fellow," he whispered softly, not wanting to startle the magnificent creature. The horse bobbed his head, as if in agreement. "I would bet, given your proud look, that you belong to Mr. Darcy."

He admired the horse for a few minutes and then turned to leave. As he exited the stall, he stopped cold at the sight of Miss Caroline Bingley, her back to him, peering around the corner of a vacant stall. An imp of mischief prompted him to keep his presence secret until he was almost upon her.

"May I help you, Miss Bingley?"

She whirled in shock, lost her balance and promptly fell onto the straw covered floor. The sound of ripping cloth rent the air, followed by her cry of surprise. As she struggled to pull herself into an upright position, he noticed a portion of her skirt hung on a protruding nail.

Nathan rushed to give her aid, which she allowed and then swatted his hand aside as soon as she stood steady on her feet. She did not even try to meet his curious gaze and began to inspect the damage to her dress, brushing off pieces of straw and dirt.

"It is a little late to clean up, do not you think?"

She raised her gaze to his and he was astonished at the amount of anger they revealed. Not one bit of remorse for whatever she'd been caught at.

"I have no idea what you are going on about. Fine gentleman you are. Sneaking up and scaring me to death and then not even apologize."

"First, I was not 'sneaking', I entered through wide open

doors," he replied in a lazy tone and propped his shoulder against the stall's frame. "If anyone was 'sneaking', it was you, peeking around the corner, spying on Mr. Darcy"

He hated to admit it, but it looked as though the various reports he'd heard were true. Miss Bingley could very well be attempting to compromise Darcy a few days before the wedding. Disappointment flooded his soul. He'd held a very real interest in her and now doubted her character. Not for the first time he was glad he'd learned to hide his true feelings while in the army. Skills further honed under the sharp eye of those in Society.

"You, sir, are no gentleman!" She shook out her skirts one final time and began walking toward the entrance that led back to the main house.

"And you," he said, "are no lady." He ignored her indignant gasp and pushed off the doorframe. In two quick strides he'd outpaced her and blocked her exit. "What were you doing here?"

She attempted to side step him, but he only placed his larger body solidly in front of her path. Frustrated, she stood still, anger rolling off her in waves.

"I heard Darcy purchased a new horse and desired to see the beast for myself," she stated and finally raised her eyes to meet his. Her clear gaze gave him pause. If she were lying, then this air of innocence was a trait she'd mastered well.

"I have it on good authority that *Mr.* Darcy bought the horse as a wedding gift for fiancé, Miss Bennet and wished no one to see it until after the ceremony," he said "And that does not explain why you were hiding in a vacant stall."

"I was not hiding!"

Nathan took a step toward her, placed a finger under her chin and forced her to raise her gaze to his. Two flags of red emblazoned her cheeks.

"You and I both know that is an outright lie. You will not attempt to trap Mr. Darcy into a situation where he must break his engagement to Miss Bennet and be forced to marry you."

"Unhand me, sir." She glared at him, her chin remaining at a haughty angle.

He ignored her request and became swept up with a ridiculous desire to fan the flames. God help him, he wanted to ruffle her feathers.

"If you are looking for a husband, you are going about it the wrong way."

"I do not know what you are talking about." A wary look crossed her face when he framed her face with both of his hands. "What…what are you doing?"

He was inexplicably drawn to the shape of her lips and wanted to lose himself in their silken texture. He wanted her attention to be solely on him, not Fitzwilliam Darcy. Slow and deliberate, never removing his gaze from hers, he leaned in. Her eyelashes fluttered down and the heat of their breath mixed.

The fact they were in the stables of his benefactor never once crossed his mind. Not until the whinny of a nearby horse pierced the haze of desire that shrouded his reasoning. Caroline must have heard it too because her eyes flew open and she stepped back, breaking the spell that had almost ended in a kiss.

What had he been thinking? If they'd been caught, not only would it ruin her reputation, but he could just as easily lose his position as Darcy's vicar.

"Forgive me. I do not know what came over me." But he did. The Rake, the seducer of women, the man he used to be had reared his ugly head and it shook him to the core. "I'll escort you back to the house where you may repair the damage before dinner."

"I am perfectly able to find my own way, Lord Nathan." Any softness he'd detected earlier disappeared behind a façade of politeness and he did not blame her one bit.

"I am well aware you can find your own way but we would not want you to lose your footing again. Who knows what might happen then?"

He knew he'd poked the bear and was glad his sainted Mother could not see him now. What was it about this young woman that brought out the worst in him? He'd never once wanted to kiss a woman this badly, not even Miss Tottingham. He'd been quite content to wait until they were married to become more intimate. There was something about Miss Bingley that made him want to ruffle her feathers. To find out if he shattered her composure as easily as she did his.

"Oh, you insufferable…" Caroline began to stalk off, muttering under her breath.

"I am sorry, Miss Bingley. Did you say something?" He grinned as he watched her storm toward the main house. When she whirled to face him, skirts flaring about her delicate ankles, he clamped his mouth tight so she would not catch him laughing. Her feathers were more than ruffled now.

"I stated you were an insufferable oaf, amongst other things." She stomped her foot. "How you vex me. And to think I waited three days for you to call—"

Her eyes widened and her mouth fell open as she realized

what she'd admitted. Without another word, she picked up her skirts and turned to run. Her admission stunned him, at the same time a thrill coursed through his veins. She'd waited for him to call. However, he could not let her leave in such a state. At best, his behavior had been uncouth, at worst, ungentlemanlike. He had to make amends, and quickly.

"Miss Bingley," he called out to her fleeing figure. Dash it all, she covered a lot of ground with those long legs. With three long strides he reached her side and stopped her flight. "Please, let me apologize."

"I will never accept your apologies, sir." She kept her face averted and refused to look at him.

"I had no right to tease you the way I did." He dropped his hand from her arm, relieved she did not move away. From that small concession he took hope she would listen to his belated counsel. "When I saw you hiding in the stable, I worried you were plotting a course of action which would result in dire consequences. I have no wish to see you ruin your life."

"How would I be ruining my life? We have but spoken a few times. You know nothing about me."

"Miss Bingley, it came to my attention you have long held aspirations of an offer from Mr. Darcy and made attempts to compromise him" – she sputtered out a vehement 'I did not!' – "Regardless, it is the general consensus amongst those who know you well. I regret being the one to speak with you in this manner, but I will not let you ruin Darcy's happiness."

"I did nothing to ruin Darcy's happiness."

"Only because I came across you first." His patience was wearing thin.

"I told you I was not doing anything wrong."

"Sneaking about the stable like a horse thief? Do not take me for a fool, Miss Bingley. I have reason to believe you were attempting to compromise Mr. Darcy."

It astounded him that she continued to pursue Darcy even when his wedding was but a few days off. Her determination was somewhat admirable, if not misguided.

"That was not my intent. I know he will never offer for me." She stared off across the meadow beside the stable. "All this started out as a nice walk in the garden. I heard the horses and remembered he purchased a mare for Elizabeth."

He believed her when she confessed she knew Darcy would never offer for her, but would someone who'd pursued a gentleman for so long, who had the patience to wait for what he reasoned had been years, give up so easily? Many a wedding had been cancelled because the bride or groom had been compromised, or eloped with someone else.

Her family and friends were caught up in all the festivities leading up to the wedding, and Darcy could be lured into a compromising position quite easily as he had numerous guests attending and would not be on his guard for a flank attack. He decided Miss Bingley needed close attention.

In silence they walked up the cobblestone path toward the house. When they reached the front garden, Nathan asked, "Miss Bingley, have you ever looked at Mr. Darcy as a man?"

"What kind of question is that?"

For a brief moment her footsteps stalled and then she hurried her pace.

"Forgive me if I have given offense. What I mean is... did you view him as a means for a comfortable life, given his vast estate and fortune, or did you ever view him as a man, with wants, fears and desires?"

"What a preposterous notion. Of course, I thought of him as a man—"

"Very well then, what is his favorite color?"

"Favorite color?" She blustered and once again attempted to move away. "How would I know that? If we had married, which you have assured me was my plan, we would have come to know each other's likes and dislikes after the wedding."

"How interesting. Miss Bennet has asked for dove grey to be part of the wedding decorations as that is Mr. Darcy's favorite color."

"Oh."

"What is his favorite dish?"

Caroline whirled around and stomped toward the house. Nathan kept pace, waiting for an answer. As they reached the front entrance, he placed a firm hand on her elbow and stopped her from entering the house. Anger blazed from her startling green eyes; her full lips pursed into a thin line.

"His favorite dish," he pressed. "Come now, Miss Bingley. You have known him for several years. Surely you must know by now what foods he likes or dislikes."

"I do not know and I do not care!" She pulled her arm from his grasp and stormed past Grieves, who'd silently opened the door. "I only wanted to look at the horse." He watched as she ascended the grand staircase, a flurry of torn silk and agitation.

"Good afternoon, Grieves."

The butler gave him a slight bob of the head, his eyes betraying a minutia of merriment.

"Mr. Darcy is down at the stables. Shall I send a footman to inform him you are here, Lord Nathan?"

"No thank you, I have already been. Can you ask Mrs. Reynolds to have Miss Bingley's maid attend her? She was exceedingly upset when she fell and tore her dress. And, can you give this list to Miss Darcy. She wanted to know which tenants were in need this month, there is a copy for Mr. Darcy as well."

"Yes, sir. I shall attend to that at once."

He gave the butler a polite nod and turned to leave. Caroline may have been returned to safety, but his heart was in great danger of being ensnared by the spoiled red-haired beauty, and that would not do. Would not do at all.

Chapter Nine

"Insufferable man!"

Caroline flung open the door to her room and promptly slammed it shut. Lord Nathan's insinuation that she meant to compromise Darcy into a marriage proposal was rich with irony, considering the very next thing he did, after insulting her, was almost kiss her.

If they'd been discovered... she shuddered at the thought. He'd have been honor bound to offer marriage. *Even if he did make an offer, I'd never accept*, she thought with a sniff. To be married to such a...a... she growled in the back of her throat. There weren't strong enough words to describe him. In her opinion, intolerable, insupportable and annoying did not come close.

She tore off her dress, uncaring that the buttons popped off and scattered across the floor. She did not want to think of him nearly kissing her. In all her one and twenty years no man had ever touched her with such intimacy. She'd felt his breath on her lips. She'd felt the heat from his body. She'd felt the world drop away.

In no way had she been prepared for the onslaught of sensations that racked her body. She'd reveled in the touch of his hands on her face. All sense of propriety fled and all she could think was kiss me, please, please, kiss me.

Not that any of that mattered. He believed she still harbored feelings for Darcy. Her face burned with embarrassment. She knew exactly to which incident he referred when he claimed she'd previously attempted to compromise the master of Pemberley and felt a keen sense of betrayal that Darcy or Charles had shared this information with a stranger. A stranger!

On occasion, she would leave her bed and walk about in her sleep. The occurrences were few and far between, however the same night Miss Elizabeth and her family had come to Pemberley, she'd had one such incident. She'd awakened in an unfamiliar hall wearing only her night gown, facing an irate Darcy. No one accepted the truth. No, they'd rather believe she skulked about the corridors in hopes of catching Darcy alone. Her character had been cast as a villain and that's all everyone wanted to see.

She knew Darcy spoke to Charles the next day and up until this moment she'd remained confident her brother informed Darcy of her propensity to walk in her sleep. Not long after that, she and Charles had an awkward discussion of what type of gentleman she should expect to court her, and although she'd wondered what made him bring the subject up, had let it escape her mind with ease. Looking back, she now realized he was warning her off Darcy.

She and Charles, along with Louisa and Mr. Hurst departed Derbyshire the following week and although her next few encounters with Darcy prior to their departure had been strained, she foolishly thought they'd put all that behind them. Even in the face of his disdain, she held tight to the dream he would pursue an alliance with her.

She ought to have known better. He'd once stated, '*My good opinion once lost, is lost forever.*'

But Charles had known the truth and in light of what Lord Nathan revealed, why had he not corrected Darcy's assumption, or at the very least, defended her? A cry caught at the back of her throat. It seemed everyone close to her, those she thought she could trust with her very life, had washed their hands of her.

She crumpled to the floor amongst the tattered ruins of her dress, wrapped her arms around her midsection and began to sob. There was no grandmamma to wipe her tears away now.

"What should I do?" she whispered to the memory of her grandmother between sobs. Oh, how she missed her unconditional love. "Who can I trust?"

As though in answer to prayer, she remembered a Bible verse grandmamma made her memorize. *Trust in the Lord with all your heart; and lean not unto thine own understanding. In all thy ways acknowledge Him, and He shall direct your path.*

A strange peace settled over her and she basked in it for a few moments, her tears slowly subsiding. Realizing how she must look, on the floor wearing only a chemise in the middle of her wrecked gown, she rose to her feet, picked up the dress and laid it across the bed. When Lucy knocked on the door a few minutes later, she was composed and ready to face her.

"Mrs. Reynolds said you needed me, Miss Caroline?"

"Yes, Lucy. I am afraid my dress is ruined beyond repair. Can you ask Mrs. Reynolds if there is someone who can make use of the material? I would hate to see such beautiful cloth go to complete waste."

"Oh, I'm sure we can find something for it. 'Tis beautiful, indeed."

She glanced at the light jade and ivory silk dress. It truly was beautiful, but what was she thinking, wearing silk during the day. Given her state of mind she was tempted to dress in somber hues and snorted out a laugh. What would everyone think if she attended the wedding in mourning colors?

It would not be far from the truth. Her whole life was slowly crumbling around her. Prior to Charles reconnecting with Jane, she'd have played hostess wherever he purchased an estate which ensured her a secure roof over her head until she married. Unless Charles and Jane did not mind her living with them, she would be forced to stay with Louisa who clearly stated last night she wanted her gone.

Mourning colors might appease her spirit, but practicality dictated she remain in the land of the living, just not as flamboyant as before. She made a mental note to find a modiste near Lambton and have some light day dresses made for the duration of her visit. In fact, that would give her the perfect excuse to avoid Pemberley over the next few days when the Bennet family descended in preparation of the wedding.

Lucy opened the wardrobe and brought out a few dresses for Caroline to choose from. With a wave of her hand she told Lucy to pick which one she thought best for the day and gazed out her window while she waited.

Within a few minutes she'd finished her toilette and sighed

when she saw what Lucy laid out for her to wear. Smoothing down the front of yet another silk dress – she shook her head in amusement – and made her way downstairs.

The next day, Caroline waited for the coachman to assist her and Lucy down from the carriage she'd borrowed from Mr. Hurst. They alighted to find themselves in front of a modest store front where Miss Darcy assured them a competent modiste kept shop.

With keen interest, she gazed up and down the busy main street of Lambton. To be sure it was not London, but the small town held a certain charm and she decided she was well pleased with the array of shops available. Lucy waited patiently as she instructed the driver to return within the hour to retrieve them and turning to Lucy stated, "Let's see what we can find."

They entered the shop and for a brief moment she felt the thrill that always accompanied her when on the hunt for something new. Row upon row of material was stacked neatly along the walls, with some bolts of cloth draped becomingly over an artful display of mannequin busts. Normally she gravitated toward deep ochre and bold jewel tones, but today she found herself perusing light muslin materials.

There were two lovely dresses on display and she admired the exquisite French knot embroidery on one gown and the design of colored wools embroidered along the hem and under the empire waistline on the other. A pattern book of needlework designs was artfully placed beside the gowns, filled with endless opportunities for women of all ages to express their style.

Instantly she knew this was the type of dress she wished to

employ. She also decided on some chestnut brown wool for a spencer and while being measured, asked if a pelisse could be made of the beautiful cream silk taffeta she'd spied upon entering the shop. She wanted to simplify, but surely a silk coat would be acceptable.

The hour she'd allotted for her and Lucy flew by and she thanked the owner of the shop, a Mrs. Braxton, who assured her she'd have the dresses ready on the morrow. About to exit the shop, she paused and asked Mrs. Braxton if there was a chapel nearby.

"Aye, Miss Bingley. There be a church in the little village between here and Pemberley."

"The name of this village?" she queried as she buttoned her gloves.

"Kympton, Miss. Oh, you'll like the vicar, a fine young gentleman. There's not a more generous soul around than Mr. Kerr, 'ceptin' Mr. Darcy hisself."

"Thank you, Mrs. Braxton. I shall see you tomorrow around afternoon, if that is acceptable."

"More'n enough time for my girls to get your dresses finished."

"I only require the embroidered yellow muslin for now. I am not in a rush for anything more, what with the ball tomorrow night, I am sure you are quite busy."

"Oh, aye. Everyone is talkin' about the ball. All them fancy dresses and such." Mrs. Braxton gave a small nod back into her shop. "It's been a busy three weeks for us here."

"I am sure it has. Mr. Darcy did not give any of us fair notice for such a momentous occasion. I shall chastise him and my brother when I return to Pemberley." Caroline stepped into the doorway and signaled the coachman. "Until tomorrow, Mrs. Braxton."

"Until then, Miss Bingley, and I thank you kindly for your business."

Lucy and Caroline climbed into the carriage and Caroline asked the driver if he could take her to the church in Kympton. Ever since she'd whispered the Bible verse of trusting the Lord, she felt an urgent need to spend some quite time in prayer and contemplation.

Within minutes the carriage pulled in front of a sizable church. She noted a large house a short distance away and beyond that a respectable stable. Darcy's vicar would have a good living here indeed.

"Wait here, Lucy. I wish to spend some time alone, if you do not mind."

Lucy bobbed her head in agreement and Caroline descended with the help of the coachman. She made her way to the front door of the chapel and was delighted to find it opened at her gentle push. She passed through the front vestibule, which branched off into two small alcoves on either side into the main chapel. Sunlight streamed through the stain glass windows, prisms of color dancing along the backs of the congregational pews which bore mute testimony to the countless number of hands that had touched the gleaming wood. At the front of the chapel, an intricately carved lectern was on the right side and an equally beautiful pulpit dominated the right.

She could well imagine her brother and Jane standing before the vicar, exchanging vows. The chapel was so beautiful, how could they not be happy with getting married here? When she married, she hoped to find a place such as this to exchange vows with her husband.

Unbidden, the image of Lord Nathan popped into her mind. She hurried to the nearest row of pews and took a seat. She came here to find peace, not re-examine her encounters with that vexing man. She did not want to meditate on his height, his unruly curls, his exceptionally long lashes, or how he invaded her dreams at night. And she definitely did not come here to think about that near kiss.

~~~ooo0ooo~~~

Nathan glanced out the window of his study and noticed an unmarked carriage in front of the church. With Mr. Darcy of Pemberley getting married in a few days, the whole area had been flooded with well-wishers and those who wished to see the sight where he would exchange vows. He never understood why the general populace needed to know every detail of what should be a most private affair and fervently hoped whoever attended the chapel would take a quick look and then be on their way.

Once more he attempted to put his thoughts into words on the paper. This Sunday, the service would be special as the banns for Mr. Darcy and Mr. Bingley were being read for the third and final time. After that, in front of what he suspected would be a full church, he had to preach a sermon. A sermon for which he was having trouble finding words.

His thoughts continuously looped back and around to one red haired beauty. She dominated his thoughts day and night and now he could not even find words to preach in front of his benefactor. This would not do. Where was his legendary control now?

He'd spent much time in prayer last night asking God to forgive him for not respecting Miss Bingley's innocence and give him peace. As a man of the cloth, he was held to a higher moral compass and although it did not happen often, at times he struggled with past behaviors.

He knew, beyond a shadow of a doubt, she was virtuous in a purely physical sense, but her heart and mind remained cloaked in mystery. In the early hours of the morning, before falling into a fitful sleep, he prayed for her soul. He prayed God would bring someone into her life, just as He brought Max to him, to lead her onto the path of righteousness.

Given his lack of sleep and jumbled state of mind, it was a good thing he had until tomorrow evening to compose his thoughts and prepare his approach. More than enough time to craft an effective apology.

He glanced through the window and noted the carriage had not departed. He placed his quill in the ink pot and pushed the papers aside. His prayers for peace and contentment were not being answered and he was fooling no one but himself by hiding away in his study. He determined to attend the church and give aid to whomever was there. Maybe the Lord would have something else for him to worry about. A good discussion on forgiving one's neighbor would be welcome respite from the continual loop of *Caroline* going through his mind.

He strode into the chapel and stopped cold in front of the pulpit. There before him, in all her glory sat Miss Caroline Bingley, head bowed in prayer. His mind stuttered to a stop. Given what had been revealed to him by various people, he never once thought this young miss would darken the door of a church voluntarily. Instantly, he was reminded of his brother's words of caution.

"Nathan, you have never judged someone by the opinions of others. Their view is skewered by their own prejudices. Give the lady a chance to prove herself. You may be pleasantly surprised."

He breathed a quick prayer for strength and knowledge of how to proceed. Obviously, the Lord saw fit for him to speak with Miss Bingley now instead of at the ball. He was about to find out if Max's quiet confidence in the good of people would stand this next test.

He advanced a few more steps, faltering only when she raised her eyes to see who approached. They widened and all color left her face. He rushed to her side in case she fainted, she'd gone so pale. He took hold of both her hands and sat beside her.

"What are you doing here?" They both asked in unison, his tone quizzical, hers weak and her countenance showing that she was visibly shaken.

"I shall go first, Miss Bingley."

"No. I am not going to stay and have you further malign my character." She looked pointedly at their joined hands and he released hers, shifting back in the pew to put more space between them. "I am of the mind that you are pursuing me and keep attempting to place me in a compromising position. First the stable and now here? Are you following me?"

His lip twitched in amusement and he tried valiantly to keep his features composed. She thought *he* was attempting to compromise *her*? It was painfully obvious she had no idea he was Darcy's vicar and a small portion of him wished to keep her in the dark, but the Christian side of his psyche would not allow it. She was a child of God and would be treated as such.

"I could accuse you of the very same thing."

"Highly unlikely as you came in after me, not before. Ergo, *you* are following *me*," she said with an elegant sniff.

He longed to laugh out loud. She was so very determined to prove him wrong.

"Let me set your mind at ease, Miss Bingley. I could not have followed you as I was already here."

"That is preposterous. There were no carriages or horses out front when we arrived."

"You are correct, because my horses and carriage are in the stable, out back."

"Horses? You cannot ride more than one at a time. What nonsense do you speak of?"

"No nonsense. My carriage and horses are in the stable behind my house."

"Your house…"

He knew understanding dawned when her eyes lit up at discovering the truth, then astonishment when her mouth formed a perfect 'o' and she gaped at him.

"You are Mr. Kerr, Darcy's new vicar!"

"Yes."

"But… you're also Lord – a Duke's son…" She floundered for words.

"I see I must share a bit of my family history."

"No, this is your private business. You do not need to… I mean…"

She began to twist her fingers and pick at the loose thread

along the seam. He'd noted before that when agitated she kept her fingers busy, which would explain why she enjoyed playing the pianoforte so much. Her fingers were engaged which allowed her mind to rest. He felt very pleased at finding some understanding of her character.

"Miss Bingley, our friendship has gotten off to a rocky start and for that I apologize. You did not deserve the treatment received by me yesterday."

"Lord Nathan, or should I call you Mr. Kerr? There is no need to apologize again.

"Yes, there is. I did not treat you with respect due a lady, and you may call me Mr. Kerr. Do not be surprised of most of Darcy's guests refer to me as Lord Nathan. There are not many outside our family circle who know I have taken orders."

"This seems so far beneath your rank, I cannot fathom why you do it."

Miss Bingley wasn't the first person to question his decisions. Strangely enough, his own family had no qualms about him pursuing a vocation in the church. It was outsiders. Those who had no idea where his heart lay that could not seem to wrap their mind around him wanting to be a vicar.

Even Miss Tottingham had disagreed with him when he shared his desire to attend seminary after giving his heart to the Lord. Within a day of his announcement, she returned his betrothal ring with a terse note written in elegant script, absolving herself from any misconstrued expectations.

Lord Nathan,

I am in returning the lovely bauble you bestowed upon me. I am truly sorry if there were any misconceptions on your part which led you to believe there was more to our relationship than being friends.

I wish you God speed in your studies.

Your friend,
L. Tottingham

He decided to take a direct approach and let God speak through his words. Heaven knew his actions were not in keeping with the moral high ground he strived for.

"As the third son, born after the heir and the second son, I knew I would never bear the title of Duke, nor would I inherit Adborough land. My life's path was my own to choose."

He shifted to face her more fully, wanting to read her reactions.

"As soon as I was able, I purchased my commission and being an excellent horseman, joined the light brigade and was promptly shipped off to France. There, I witnessed events that made me question man's humanity. I did things no man should ever have to do in order to survive. When I was finally sent home, I was a broken man, physically and spiritually."

He paused to gather his thoughts. She laid a gloved hand on his forearm, her touch light.

"Please, Lord Nathan. Do not go any further if this distresses you. I have no right to question your choices." Her soft tone humbled him.

"Miss Bingley," he continued with a small smile. "I asked God to guide my words, and I feel this is what he wants you to hear. Will you let me continue?"

After a slight hesitation, she nodded her assent.

"I returned to England bitter and dissolute. Max helped

me find my way again. I had almost completed my seminary studies when Darcy offered me this living in Kympton."

"So many young men have been lost over there and the war is not over yet. At times I fear the French will visit us on our doorstep."

"The Duke of Wellington is keeping Napoleon very busy in France. We are safe, here in England," he assured her.

He gathered her hands in his and simply held them. Her cheeks tinged a becoming pink and her eyelashes fluttered down to caress them. He fought the desire to kiss her yet again and glanced up at the cross, silently asking God to forgive him for his very human thoughts.

"I lost a brother in France."

She raised face, her eyes shimmering with unshed tears. Startled, he dropped her hands.

"I am so sorry. No one told me you had another brother."

"Henry was the eldest, named after my father. I miss him so much. He would bring me sweet treats whenever I was sent to my room." She turned to look at him and a small smile ghosting her lips. "I know you will not be surprised by this, but I was often sent to my bed without supper. Mother did not know how to handle my 'high spirits'."

He choked back a laugh. Miss Bingley may joke about this now, but as a child, she would have been angry and confused if she thought she was being unjustly punished.

"Henry always made sure I did not waste away in my tower, as he liked to call it. When the war started, he was too young to sign up, but as soon as he was able, he joined the light infantry. We had no idea where he was, or whether he was alive or dead. Almost a year passed before the War Office informed our family that within a few weeks of arriving in France, he'd been killed. Papa was devastated. Henry meant everything to him and he died shortly after we received notice."

She pulled out her reticule and fumbled inside the pouch. Finally, she stopped and sighed out, "Where is my Steward of the Linen Cupboard when I need him?"

"Your Steward?" Nathan queried, reaching inside his coat for a fresh handkerchief and handing it to her.

"Yes," she laughed softly. "Charles called himself that the other day when he gave Jane and me handkerchiefs. We were both crying tears of joy during our last visit."

"Ah," he nodded in understanding. "Everybody should have a Steward of the Linen Cupboard for those very reasons."

He watched her twist the handkerchief with slight agitation, which brought him back to the first thing he'd wondered when he found her in the sanctuary.

"Miss Bingley, might I enquire as to why you came here today? I realize you did not expect to find me, but you must have had reason to enter God's house."

"You are going to think me very foolish."

"When a person seeks truth, they are never foolish. They are wise."

"That's something grandmamma would say if she were here."

"Your grandmother sounds like a wise woman."

"She was." Caroline stuffed the handkerchief into her reticule and sighed heavily. "I am at a crossroad. Charles is marrying Jane and I hate to impose on them as newlyweds, but I can no longer impinge upon Louisa's hospitality. She has confessed she is with child and requires my room."

"I see. What of your mother?"

"Mother passed away a few years ago and we sold the house soon after. All we have left are Papa's textile factories, which Charles manages through a competent Foreman and the shipping business near Liverpool. I do have an aunt in Scarborough, but there is no place to call my own," she said with a small shrug of her shoulders.

"You are indeed at a crossroad. May I pray with you as you seek guidance from the Lord?"

She hesitated only briefly and then nodded. Nathan did not waste a single moment. He bowed his head and prayed softly, "Father God, thank you for bringing Miss Bingley to Your house. Guide her in the decisions she needs to make and help her realize that You love her, unconditionally. Amen."

He wondered what exactly was going on in this beautiful woman's life. Like himself, on the surface she had so much, yet maybe she was barren in her soul, as he had been before seeking God's face.

Chapter Ten

Caroline handed her pelisse, gloves and reticule to Lucy who immediately took them upstairs to her room. The ride home from Kympton had given her time to think about Lord Nathan's revealing conversation. That he was a kind man evidenced by the way he treated others, the exception being her.

For some reason, he insisted on antagonizing her until she lost all decorum and ranted at him like a lunatic. Yet today, when he found her in the church praying, he'd been the soul of compassion. She may have dreamed of Lord Nathan, the Rake courting her, but the idea of Mr. Kerr, the vicar of Darcy courting her gave her pause. He confused her greatly.

There was much activity in the house as the Bennet's had finally arrived, along with the Gardiner's. She passed by the drawing room and heard her name called out.

"Caroline. Come and join us for tea."

She looked into the room and saw Jane, Elizabeth and Georgiana grouped together near the fireplace, a tea service and small sandwiches set before them. Her stomach rumbled and she realized she'd not eaten since breaking her fast that morning and supper would not be until much later in the evening. Mrs. Reynolds informed her she would be setting out a buffet as more guests were expected to arrive and they could eat at their leisure.

She joined the ladies and after securing two small sandwiches and a cup of tea, settled in and listened as the three of them discussed wedding plans. Instantly, she was reminded of Lord Nathan's censure of her not knowing Darcy's likes and dislikes.

"I understand dove grey is one of the colors being featured in your wedding decorations."

"Yes, it is." Elizabeth tilted her head and gave her a curious look. "How did you come by that knowledge? We are attempting to keep this secret even from Darcy."

"My source shall remain nameless. I would not want them to get into any trouble. I never knew he liked dove grey."

"It is one of his favorites," Georgiana enthused. "His valet is forever complaining how foggy his wardrobe looks." She giggled. "He has to force him to intersperse other colors into his waistcoats and overcoats. Fitz draws the line at pastels. Refuses to wear anything resembling a flower."

"Charles has an affinity for blue," Jane stated softly.

"Yes, he does." Caroline affirmed. She knew there was one thing she could share with her soon-to-be-sister that would make her very happy. "That affinity became stronger after he met you. He professed God himself placed the blue from heaven in your eyes."

Jane blushed and bowed her head. She exhibited such a soft, gentle soul and Caroline now understood why her brother loved her deeply. The fact that the elder Bennet sister had tried to find good in both her and Louisa, even when they'd sought to undermine her connection with Charles, told her how blessed they were to have this woman join their family.

"And you, Georgiana. Do you have any surprises awaiting your brother?" she asked.

"Oh no, I dare not. Fitz is very precise in everything he does. I might muck up the wheels if I tried to surprise him."

"Darling Georgiana, there is nothing you could do to lose his favor." She gave a light laugh, and wondered at the slight grimace that crossed Georgiana's face. It passed so quickly she thought she must have imagined it. "He intimated strongly, when we were all at Netherfield, that you were an accomplished young woman. You may recall that conversation, Elizabeth. You were there."

"It has been long known to me how much your brother respects and admires you, Georgiana. He is extremely proud to call you his sister," Elizabeth said.

"I… th..thank you," her stammer becoming evident as she blushed at their words. "I confess I worry he only sees me as a young foolish girl."

All the women seated with her broke out in objection.

"Nonsense."

"You are a fine young woman."

"He is so very proud of you."

Georgiana held up her hands and laughed. "Thank you. I am grateful for your vote of confidence." There was a noise in the hall and she glanced toward the open door. "Mrs. Bennet, Miss Bennet's, please come join us for tea."

Elizabeth leaned forward and touched Georgiana's arm.

"We are going to be family and there are still too many Miss Bennet's for mama's liking. Please call my sisters by their Christian names. I am sure Mama will not mind."

"Mind? Good heavens, no. Why would I mind?" Mrs. Bennet bustled into the room and looked for a place to sit. She eyed the empty space beside Caroline on the small couch and made a point of moving to a chair opposite her. Apparently, Mrs. Bennet had not forgiven her previous conduct toward Jane last year. She could not speak for Louisa, but she had much work to do on her own.

"Mrs. Bennet," she addressed the lady directly. "Are you looking forward to the ball tomorrow night?"

At first, she thought she'd receive no answer, but after a few long seconds Mrs. Bennet replied, although her manner remained stiff and formal.

"I'm looking forward to the ball. So many dignified people attending, as well as those not so dignified, I am sure." She cast her eyes upon Caroline at the last statement. Mrs. Bennet was not known for her subtlety and this had not changed in a year. "I'm sure there'll be plenty of young men for my girls to dance with."

"I am sure there will be."

"Oh yes. The Duke of Adborough looks to be a fine young man. He would partner up quite nicely with Kitty." She glanced at Katherine as she spoke. "Sit up straight, Kitty. You'll never attract a gentleman if you slouch so."

"Yes, mama," came the dutiful reply.

And so, it began. Mrs. Bennet vacillated between rhapsodizing about the guests, the house, the grounds to chastising her daughters, or rather daughter as she seemed to ignore Mary, of coughing too much, or eating too much cake. Her one-woman monologue came to an abrupt end when her sister-in-law, Mrs. Gardiner, entered the room.

Caroline noted Elizabeth give her aunt a small roll of her eyes when she entered and with one, "Good afternoon, Fanny. I see you are in fine form today," Mrs. Bennet ceased speaking almost completely.

That Mrs. Bennet was a trifle bit in awe of her brother's wife made Caroline more inclined to know her better.

Mrs. Gardiner seated herself next to Jane and turned to face Georgiana.

"I must concur with my sister-in-law; you do have a lovely estate. I took a walk through the glass enclosure your brother was constructing when we were here last August. What a delight. Your gardener took time out of his busy schedule to show me around. I am amazed at the number of vegetables and fruits your cook has access to over the winter months."

"Darcy spoke of it when it was being constructed, but I have never seen it. Hopefully I can before we all leave." Caroline felt a pang when she spoke the words. After her time here at Pemberley, she had no clue where she'd live. Netherfield Park, Grosvenor Street or some hovel she rented out until she found suitable lodgings.

"There is time now, before we have to dress for dinner, if you like." Georgiana offered.

"Yes, I would like that very much."

A few minutes later both women strolled along the path that wound through the arboretum beside the glass enclosure, bundled up in warm coats and gloves. The younger girl practically sparkled as she talked about the different species of trees and growing conditions, praising her brother for his foresight in planning for future generations. Caroline felt deep regret that she'd never taken the time to really know Darcy's sister.

"We have much in common, Georgiana. We both want the very best for our brothers."

"You are always so poised and confident, Miss Bingley. I did not think we had anything in common."

"Stuff and nonsense. Remember, we are but four years apart in age and have our love of music as a sisterly bond."

"I feel as though we could be good friends." Impulsively, Georgiana looped her arm through Caroline's. "Elizabeth already feels like a sister to me and who could not love Jane. You shall become one of my dear friends in time. I just know it."

"I would like to think that." They passed by a towering oak, its leaves tenaciously clinging to outstretched branches. "What else captures your interest?"

"I love to paint watercolors. Do you like to paint?"

"I do but none of my attempts resemble what I sought to capture. Charles once stated my peonies on canvas looked like our dog had walked through a most colorful mud puddle. I must satisfy my creative outlet with embroidery and the pianoforte."

Georgiana laughed at her descriptions and the rest of their walk was spent in lively conversation. When relaxed, Darcy's sister surprised her with her wit and vivacity. It was too bad she was such a shy soul when faced with large groups of people. There had to be a way to bring this young woman out of her shell. She resolved to think of a way to do that without encroaching upon their budding friendship.

"What do you do when your home is not being invaded by family and friends?"

"I like to visit our tenants. What with Christmas fast approaching and the cold weather setting in, some families struggle. With the help of Mr. Kerr, we created a list and shall take baskets of food and small gifts for the children."

"Would not your steward take care of those things?"

"No." Georgiana looked surprised by her question. "They are not his tenants, but ours. It is our responsibility to ensure their safe keeping. Now that Fitz is marrying Elizabeth, the duty will fall upon her." She lifted her shoulder in a graceful shrug. "It is what we do."

The next afternoon, Caroline exited the modiste shop, extremely satisfied with the work of Mrs. Braxton and her girls. Not only had they completed the embroidered dress, but also the coordinating spencer and Lucy would attend tomorrow for the rest of her purchase. She felt a small regret that after the wedding she would not be within easy access of Mrs. Braxton's establishment, for her eye to detail was impressive.

She glanced up and down the busy street and seeing their coachman, signaled him. He jumped down from the coach and was about to lower the step so she and Lucy could enter, when a familiar voice stopped her.

"A lovely day for a drive, do not you agree, Miss Bingley?"

She turned to face Lord Nathan, a lopsided smile turning up one corner of his firm mouth. A jaunty beaver hat sat upon his unruly curls and he looked exceedingly handsome in his dark overcoat that did nothing to hide his broad expanse of shoulders. Steele grey eyes sparkled with untold mischief and she imagined his nanny must have seen that look many times as he grew up with two older brothers.

Lucy bobbed a quick curtsy and Caroline murmured, "Lord Nathan," along with a polite nod. "I am sure it would, if I had the time. As it is, we must return to Pemberley and prepare for tonight's ball."

"That's exactly what I wish to speak with you about."

"The ball?"

"Yes, the ball, among other things. Would you allow me to drive you back to Pemberley so we may speak further?"

"I cannot be alone with you, Lord Nathan," she raised a hand to her throat in dismay. "How would Lucy get back to Pemberley?"

"Come now, Miss Bingley. Where is that scrap of a girl who was forever being banished to the tower because she had 'high spirits'? In London, young ladies go for drives with young men all the time without a chaperone."

"They do, but that is during fine weather, when the top is down and all can see the couple are not engaged in anything risqué. And we, sir, are not in London."

"Quite true." He paused as if in deep thought. "I propose that your driver and lady's maid follow. Although the top stays up so we do not freeze from the wind, I will never let my carriage out of their sight. Can you agree with that?"

She paused for a few moments, at war with herself. Lord Nathan made her heart trip along a little faster, but she had a plan for her life and it did not involve marrying a vicar and being squirreled away in Derbyshire. Her goal, ever since her first class at Mrs. Rombough's School for Elegant Young Ladies, had been to secure a toe hold in the *ton*. Being distracted by a handsome scoundrel, such as Lord Nathan, did not fit into her equation.

Yet, after their encounter at the chapel the other day, she felt a keen affinity with him. It was as though she'd met someone who understood her better than even her siblings. Giving in to what she equated with temptation, she nodded assent.

"Excellent." He offered his arm to Caroline and Lucy headed to the other carriage. When Lord Nathan lifted her into the curricle, she felt the tense and flex of his muscles and her breath caught in her throat at his familiarity. Hopefully no one of consequence witnessed his brazen behavior. Within minutes, he'd tucked the lower half of her body with a warm woolen blanket and moved around to his side of the carriage.

Before Lord Nathan climbed into the carriage, an elderly lady stopped him on the street.

"Mr. Kerr. I am so glad I saw you today."

"Miss Braithwaite." He politely tipped his hat at her. "How is your sister doing?"

"She's doing poorly, however the broth you and Miss Darcy brought by the other day helped so much. If only she could keep down anything with meat."

"My housekeeper's broth is the best she could have right now, after prayer. Mrs. Crenshaw said she'd make some soft bread for your aunt to dip in the broth. She also thought she might like a bit of cheese as well. May I bring them by tomorrow?"

"Oh, God bless you, Mr. Kerr. You're welcome

anytime."

"God bless you too, Miss Braithwaite, until tomorrow."

With that he climbed into the curricle and with a snap of his wrists, the horses began a quick pace through the town toward Pemberley.

"I am glad you agreed to join me. I am off to Pemberley to pick up my brother."

"Doesn't he have his own carriage and horse?"

"Yes, but sometimes it's easier for if I pick him up in a non-descript carriage. People tend to gawk at the ducal crest."

"I suppose they would. The highest ranking noble in this part of Derbyshire is Darcy's uncle, The Earl of Matlock."

"Quite. Although there will be more crested carriages on these roads later today as more guests arrive for the ball."

There was a time when the mention of so many titled persons in attendance would have caused her much stress alongside intense satisfaction, but now that did not even merit a raised eyebrow.

"I am so looking forward to the ball. Charles, or course, is looking for any reason to hold Jane in his arms and I have it on good authority that Darcy has asked the orchestra to play the waltz."

"Then, I shall have to make sure you mark my name next to the waltz."

"I..." Surprised by his flirtatious suggestion, she fumbled to answer. "That is... yes. Thank you."

"You may wish to hold on to that thank you. You have no idea if I can waltz or not."

In spite of herself, she giggled like a schoolgirl. Of what she'd seen of Lord Nathan's physique and how he carried himself, she had no doubt he would waltz with perfection.

"Laugh if you must, Miss Bingley, but I have been away from the ballrooms of London for nigh unto four years and the waltz only made its debut this past Season. I may well tread on your toes and ruin your slippers."

"Then I suggest you practice in your room today," came her pert reply. She determined to find Georgiana and ask if she knew how to perform the scandalous dance. If not, the two of them would be very busy in the music room this afternoon.

They drove on and spoke of generalities, of the weather, of the upcoming wedding but sooner than expected, Lord Nathan brought the conversation around to what he still obviously believed was her misguided determination to marry someone of the *ton*. For all his frustrating qualities, and there were more than she cared to number, he challenged her to think and their debate became lively.

"Miss Bingley, life is like climbing a mountain. We all start at the bottom and our goal is to reach the top. You have been attempting to reach the summit by every means possible – except by climbing. You will not achieve a sense of accomplishment until you decide to put on sturdy boots and begin to walk."

"What's wrong with trying other means? There are many who have sought to better themselves through marriage, and believe me, there are many of the nobility who have married beneath them because they squandered their family fortunes away. I find it ironic that a Peer can marry beneath them and somehow, it's swept under the rug, but if a person like me, who comes from 'trade', endeavors to create a better life for their family, we are looked upon as nothing better than rats attempting to crawl out from the gutter. The hypocrisy frustrates me. No, it more than frustrates me, it enrages me at times."

"Bravo. Your eyes are wide open, so I challenge you. Why do you want to marry a Peer? Will their title love you? If you have a title, but not the respect of your husband, what have you accomplished?"

"You make it sound like I am never going to succeed in securing a successful marriage."

"I did not say that. I desire you look at the summit of your mountain with clear eyes. I want you to strive for things that bring you joy.

"What would bring me exceedingly great joy is for you to cease this conversation."

"Now where's the fun in that?"

"You have only known me a scant few weeks and know nothing of my dreams and goals."

"Ah, but that is where you are wrong. I came from the place you are in."

She twisted in her seat to face him, her mouth opening and closing without a sound coming out. How preposterous, and she stated as much.

"How preposterous. You have never come from the place I am. You are the son of a Peer. I'd wager my dowry that even while your reputation lay in tatters about you, invitations still poured into your house. Please stop me if I am wrong."

"Oh no, Miss Bingley, you are not wrong. My statement was in reference to my soul. No amount of parties, or drink, or fast women cured the darkness which festered deep within my soul. Only God took all that away and threw it as far as the

East is from the West. Can you declare such a peace in your life?"

She turned back to face the road, grateful that Pemberley was fast approaching. Lord Nathan not only made her think, but question where her life was heading. She had no answers for him because she did not know. She'd fought long and hard to attain her goals, which had been ripped from her grasp, and she no longer knew what peace was.

They pulled to the front of the house and as he took her hand to help her down from the carriage, he said softly, "I pray for you, Miss Bingley. I pray you give God a chance to bring peace into your life."

She released his hand and hurried into the house, belatedly realizing she'd not even said a proper thank you or good bye.

Elsewhere at Pemberley...

"Brother, may I ask you something before you leave on your wedding trip?"

"Of course, you may."

Darcy, seated at his desk, watched as Georgiana approach. Although she still had a layer of shyness surrounding her, he'd caught glimpses of the fun-loving girl she'd been before that fateful day at Ramsgate. Watching her interact with the other ladies was like watching a beautiful butterfly slowly emerge from its protective cocoon. Next year would be her first Season in London and he no longer feared how she would fare. His little sister was growing up.

She settled into the chair facing his desk and smoothed down her skirts before raising her gaze to his. At times she looked so much like their mother it hurt his heart, although she had the hazel eyes of the Darcy family, not the startling blue of the Matlock clan.

"What did you wish to ask, poppet?" He asked, using his favorite name for her.

"As you know, since Mrs. Annesley has gone on to care for her mother, I am without a companion and I am not keen on departing Pemberley to stay with Aunt and Uncle Matlock."

"There are not many options, Georgiana, other than Aunt Catherine – and we all know you do not want to stay there."

"No. Aunt Catherine places too many frivolous strictures on my activities. She doesn't allow me out of the nursery until the afternoon has almost passed. I think she's forgotten that I am almost ten and eight."

"I agree. Then what did you have in mind? It had better be good. I won't allow you to ramble about the grounds unescorted, even if Pemberley is the safest place for you."

"I have thought about this a lot and over the past week I have become close to one of the ladies in attendance. Their nature has changed and I am pleased to call her friend. If she's willing, I'd like to invite her to stay while you and Elizabeth are away." Georgiana's eyes were bright with excitement.

"Who did you have in mind?"

"Miss Caroline Bingley."

Darcy never thought his sister would ever surprise him again, but she had. He leaned back in the chair, steepled his fingers together and tapped his bottom lip, deep in thought. Although he'd never have believed it possible, Miss Bingley had shown a remarkable change of character. So much so even his darling Elizabeth commented upon it.

"I'll think on it, Georgiana and let you know after we've

had tea this afternoon."

"Thank you, Fitz!" She jumped up from the chair, hurried around the desk to throw her arms around his neck. Her spontaneous hug shocked him and unbidden tears sprang to his eyes. Since Ramsgate she'd eschewed any form of familial intimacy and if Caroline Bingley could bring his little sister safely out of her shell, he'd be forever in her debt. He had much to think upon.

Chapter Eleven

From an archway, Nathan surveyed the ballroom, searching for Miss Bingley. The room slowly filled with guests and soon the cacophony of voices rose in tandem with the heat of many bodies. His brother joined him and they stood together, nodding politely at those who wished them well.

"I see you are much distracted." Max murmured quietly. "Could it be you wait for a certain red-haired beauty to arrive?"

"There is not much I can hide from you, is there?"

"No little brother. To me, you are an open book. Ah, I see Darcy. I'll speak with you later."

Max left his side and Nathan glanced back toward the main entrance and there she stood. Aphrodite had deigned to come down amongst mankind. Her gown, overlaid by a thin gossamer sheath dotted with diamonds, shimmered with her every movement beneath the glow of the chandeliers. Her hair had been skillfully woven with tiny crystals and one lock curled around her neck to caress her shoulder. Desire to follow the length of that lock with his lips hit him with swift precision.

He noticed her glance about the room and hesitate and was

struck with clarity of thought that she had nowhere to go. Her brother, surrounded by his fiancé, her family and Darcy's family, had his back to her and was completely unaware of her entrance. The sister, Mrs. Hurst stood beside her husband, deep in conversation with one of the other guests and given the fact she'd basically thrown Miss Bingley from her home, he doubted she'd be inclined to approach them.

He wasted no time and cleaved his way through the crowd. He was about ten feet from her when she finally spied him approaching. For one brief moment he held her gaze and was startled by the stark loneliness in her eyes. She snapped open her gold lace fan and brought it up to her face, creating an effective barrier from his scrutiny. The pomander she always wore swung back and forth with each frantic flick of the wrist.

Strangely pleased at her discomfort, he stopped by the refreshment table and filled two punch glasses with lemonade. He liked the thought she was as off balance in his presence as he was in hers. Emerald eyes, filled with wariness, watched him approach.

"Good evening, Miss Bingley," he said with a polite bow.

"Good evening, Lord Nathan," she replied and lowered the fan to give him a slight curtsy.

"May I claim the first dance?" He offered her one of the glasses of punch.

"Yes, you may." She took a sip of her punch and wrinkled her nose in surprise. "Oh, that is tart."

He sipped his and agreed. "Darcy loves fresh lemonade and doesn't care much for sugar. Take your time. The drink will grow on you."

"I well know how he doesn't like sugar. I'd just forgotten

how sour his lemonade can be. There will be a run on his sherry before the night is through."

He ignored the rise of jealousy at her casual reminder of how well she knew Darcy and instead laughed at her candor. "You may be right. I have also discovered the waltz will be played before supper. May I be so bold as to write my name on your card for that as well?"

At her blush he smiled and took the tiny card from her hand, pleased to see it was empty. He was sure before the night was over, her card would be filled. Only a fool would not want to dance with such a beauty as she.

The musicians prepared for the first dance and he lifted the unfinished drink from her gloved hand and placed both their glasses on a sideboard a few feet away. When he returned he held out his arm, liking the way she fit nicely against his side, and escorted her to the ballroom floor.

"Have you been told how lovely you look this evening?" He asked as they came together in the dance. During the next sequence, she replied, "No, and thank you for the compliment."

They separated and moved down the line.

"It's very easy to compliment you."

"You would be the first. I am not usually so favored."

Not so favored? He found that difficult to believe. Beautiful women always received compliments.

"Then, the men in London are fools."

"Fools or not, the men in London, or shall I say, the men in polite society pay little attention to our family."

He moved the conversation to more general topics and all too soon the set was finished and he reluctantly escorted her to where his brother Max stood, conversing with Viscount Stanhope. His lip curled at the sight of the older man and thoughts of turning around and whisking her to the other side of the ballroom ran through his mind. He knew his manner should be more Christ-like, but Stanhope was a lewd individual and there'd been many rumors attached to his behavior, not all complimentary. However, both men had seen them so they continued forward.

"Viscount Stanhope, may I introduce you to Miss Caroline Bingley. Her brother is marrying Miss Jane Bennet alongside Mr. Darcy and his affianced, Miss Elizabeth Bennet."

"Miss Bingley, pleasure to see you again." Max gave Caroline a nod of greeting, which she returned with a small curtsy.

"You're from up North, aren't you, you and your brother? I heard your family's in trade." Viscount Stanhope said the word 'trade' with mild disgust while his gaze roamed freely over her face and body. "Not that it would stop a man from enjoying your company."

Caroline stiffened slightly at his contempt of trade and ill-disguised insult, and without cutting the Viscount directly, turned to watch others enjoying the second set of dances. Thankfully, Max skillfully steered Stanhope into a conversation of a horse he wished to purchase at Tattersalls.

"I know exactly which filly you speak of Adborough. Fine horse, young, never been ridden." Stanhope's beady eyes returned to Caroline's form as he spoke to Max. "You know what that's like, eh, to feel firm flesh between your legs."

Nathan's hand curled into a tight fist. How dare he insult Miss Bingley in such a fashion, and in front of a Duke, no less?

Max must have sensed his brother's anger because he stopped the Viscount before he said anything further.

"That is quite enough, Stanhope."

He delivered the sentence in a quiet voice, his gaze narrowed. Nathan knew that look. His father used it often when disciplining them and Max seemed to have perfected the chilling glance as well. He and his brother George also knew the quieter the voice, the deeper the anger.

The Viscount swiveled his head away from Caroline and stared, slack jawed at Max. His face flushed a ruddy red and he snarled out, "Do not know why you're upset about a chit from trade, unless you're keeping her for yourself." He passed one more lecherous look over Caroline before turning away.

Nathan took an involuntary step toward his retreating back but Max's hand on his forearm forestalled him.

"Not here," he said in a low undertone and then in a louder voice, "Miss Bingley, would you do me the honor of the next dance?"

Caroline nodded in ascent, a somewhat dazed look on her face, the magnitude of the Viscount's insult hitting her full force. Nathan fought the rising tide of his anger. There was a part of him that wanted to call the Viscount out for his actions, but he was neither her betrothed, nor family.

Max escorted Caroline to the dance floor and he watched impotently from the sidelines as his brother slowly cajoled a smile from her. Before their set ended, Lord Waverly joined him.

"Kerr, I do not see you for years at a time and in the last month I have run into you twice. How are you, old man?"

"I am well. I did not think you'd come this far north for

the sake of a friend's wedding. You do not like to leave London."

The Marquis laughed. "The Season has wound down and there's absolutely nothing going on in Town, plus, this is the most talked about wedding of the year. Who would not want to attend and see the proud Mr. Darcy get married?"

Max and Caroline returned to their group and the Marquis gave her a polite bow. "Miss Bingley. What a happy occasion for you and your family. Hurst told me your brother is marrying the sister of Darcy's affianced."

"He and my brother met the Bennet sisters when we were at his estate in Hertfordshire."

"They say you can find true love anywhere, but who would have suspected Hertfordshire." He laughed at his own joke and Caroline smiled back at him. "Miss Bingley, may I have this next dance? I'd like to get to know you better."

"Thank you, Lord Dorchester." She rested her satin covered hand on his arm and Nathan once again watched as another man took her to the floor. This time she laughed gaily and had a livelier step. It did not matter the dance was more energetic, all he knew was that she hadn't glanced his way once since their dance and it unsettled him.

"Stanhope has the intelligence of a potato," Max stated once Caroline was out of ear shot. "He ogles all women and his wife probably boxes his ears when they are home because of it."

"That was more than ogling. He practically stripped her bare before us and then he as good as called her a whore. I wanted to physically assault him."

"Sadly, he voiced the opinion most of the *ton* feel. It's not right, I know," he said quickly when Nathan would have protested. "You know this for a fact. You are becoming too involved with a woman you have known for only a few weeks. What happened to spending time in prayer before committing yourself?"

Nathan shoved a hand through his hair in frustration. "I have prayed. I prayed and waited for an answer and it's like the gates of heaven have closed on me. I have found no peace, nor have I found any answers. Only more questions."

"Then I would think you are avoiding the truth. You have received your answer and do not like it." His interest suddenly veered to the other side of the ballroom. "Excuse me. I promised this set to Miss Georgiana."

He quickly strode away and approached Darcy's shy young sister. There was nothing untoward in Max's attention, but something about the way he behaved triggered the memory of a previous comment. *I love her without question, but she hasn't really experienced anything beyond her home.*

Nathan decided to stroll among the guests. If he stood around waiting for Miss Bingley to return to his side, tongues would wag more than they already did. As it was gossips would already be busy tittering about her activities. So far, she'd danced with a Lord, a Duke and now a Marquis. If they were in London and this was the beginning of the Season, she'd be declared a moderate success.

His ramblings brought him to where Darcy, Bingley and the Bennet family were situated. Polite introductions were made and it amused him that Darcy referred to him as 'Mr. Kerr, my vicar' when speaking to Mr. and Mrs. Bennet and their two unmarried daughters.

Mrs. Bennet pushed toward him, dragging the daughter who did not scowl so much with her. He thought her name was Catherine, but then maybe she was Mary. The introductions had been completed so quickly he wasn't quite sure.

"Mr. Kerr, it's so lovely to meet Mr. Darcy's vicar. How do you like Derbyshire?" She tugged the girl closer. "Come now, Kitty, be polite to Mr. Darcy's vicar."

He realized Mrs. Bennet was sizing him up as a potential son-in-law and glanced down at Miss Catherine Bennet. Eyes wide with fear, her mouth moved but no words came out and instantly he felt sorry for her.

Miss Elizabeth stepped forward. "Mamma, Mr. Kerr has come as he promised this next country dance to me. I am sorry Mr. Kerr; I forgot to check my dance card."

He admired her quick thinking with regard to her mother's actions, but did not like the blatant untruth, even if it were small lie. He thought to correct her, but she'd already laid her hand upon his forearm and they proceeded to the dance floor.

"Forgive me, Lord Nathan, for forcing you to go along in a lie," she whispered as they danced. "Mamma can be quite... I sought to save her some embarrassment."

"Mr. Darcy does not mind that you are standing up with me?"

"No," she softly chuckled. "It was he who encouraged me to be so forward. He's had his share of dealing with my mother. She's still of the mindset that she has five daughters to marry off. I think once she is settled with only two at home, she may relax and enjoy herself again."

The remainder of the dance was spent in general

conversation and he admired Miss Elizabeth's quick intellect. Darcy indeed had found a gem in this woman. They returned to her group and he noticed Miss Bingley had also joined them and was in conversation with Darcy. Thankfully, her brother Charles had taken Miss Catherine to the dance floor, so he was spared further matchmaking schemes from Mrs. Bennet.

He found his attention straying to Miss Bingley. She laughed at something Darcy said and teasingly tapped his arm with her fan. It seemed she was ready to enjoy everyone's company but his. He'd watched her bloom as she'd danced with the Marquis and then Max, and now she veritably glowed whilst talking to Darcy, and suddenly he knew. He knew he wanted her attention to be on him, and only him. They announced the supper set and Miss Bingley glanced at him, her expression wary.

"Miss Bingley, I believe you promised me this dance."

"Yes, I did."

Once they were on the dance floor, he took her hand in his and slid his arm around her waist, relishing the feel of her graceful form next to his. They began to move in time with the music and the desire to pull her even closer became almost unbearable.

He'd been an utter recluse for over three years and not only was he dancing a second time with a woman nobody in polite circles knew, but it was also the scandalous waltz. He may as well have stood in the middle of the ballroom and declared himself as far as anyone watching was concerned.

"You seem to be enjoying yourself." He stated, trying without much luck to regain his equilibrium.

"Yes. There are some very fine gentlemen in attendance."

They moved around the floor in perfect unison.

"Lord Dorchester seemed much taken by you."

"He has much to be admired for."

Jealousy gripped him. Was she still only concerned with someone's title or wealth?

"Dorchester is known to enjoy the company of many without making any commitments."

"I did not require a commitment from him. At least he made sure I was returned to my brother's side."

"Very likely so you would not get the wrong idea."

"I did not think he'd propose marriage after one dance, my Lord." Her green eyes blazed up at him. He knew he'd overstepped his boundaries, but could not seem to stop.

"No, he would not. He will marry someone who can advance *his* family's name."

Her quick intake of breath told him his comment had hit the mark and they danced the remainder of the waltz in silence. He was not surprised when Caroline refused to take his arm to be escorted to supper. He'd been a fool. No, that was too soft. He'd been an ass.

Chapter Twelve

With so many in attendance, Caroline remained hopeful no one would take note of her slipping out of the ballroom. All she needed was a few moments of uninterrupted peace and quiet. Her thoughts were all jumbled after her dance with Lord Nathan.

She'd gone only a few paces when she heard footsteps behind her. Turning, she prepared to excuse herself.

"Forgive me, —*Oh*, it's you."

"Yes, it's me."

She should have known. Only one person would disturb any sense of peace she hoped to find. He not only invaded her thoughts at inopportune times, but now he physically dogged her heels.

"Were you expecting someone else, Miss Bingley? Perchance the Marquis of Dorchester, or maybe even Mr. Darcy?"

"Keep your voice down. Someone may hear you and totally misconstrue what you are saying."

She darted a glance down the hall toward the open door

to the ballroom. He advanced, not stopping until he was close enough to loom over her, his mouth set in a grim line.

"I know for a fact the Marquis came this way only a few minutes ago. Immediately I ascertained you might follow and attempt to compromise him. Desperate times call for desperate measures, and you are feeling the pinch over where you will reside in the next few months."

"I did no such thing," she protested.

The Marquis could have pranced by her in a bright red suit and she would not have noticed. All of her attention had been focused on the infuriating man before her, even when she'd danced with the charming Lord Dorchester.

"Admit you followed him."

"I. Admit. Nothing."

The sound of voices from the ballroom reminded her of their precarious position and she pressed against the wall, determined to stay out of direct view from the doorway. Lord Nathan turned at the sound of those voices and then back at her.

"This won't do. Come with me," he said, shaking his head.

He placed a firm hand beneath her elbow and directed their steps down the hall. She attempted to pull her arm free, but he only tightened his grip. Other than calling for help and bring attention to the fact they were alone and unchaperoned; she had no other option than to walk with him.

They reached the music room and he guided her in, leaving the door open. She advanced a few steps and then whirled to face him, her temper simmering below the surface of other volatile sentiments she could not quite put a finger on. He stood framed in the door and his gaze, inscrutable as always, pinned her in place like a captured butterfly.

"What? You look at me as though I have spots on my face." A growl of frustration escaped her lips. "What are you looking at?"

"I am waiting for horns to sprout through the top of your head."

"You're what? Horns? How could you..." she sputtered, unable to complete another sentence in light of his statement.

"Admit it, Miss Bingley. You sought to make an advantageous marriage, regardless of whom the groom was nigh unto three years. Your hope for Darcy has fled, so you look toward another."

"I have done no such..." Her words trailed off as he stepped closer.

For a moment the only sound in the room was the soft swish of silk from her skirt as she retreated, stopping only when the pianoforte was at her back. He advanced until the edge of her skirt brushed the top of his shoes. She pressed further against the pianoforte and tried to glance over his shoulder. A wry smile lifted the corner of his firm lips when he noted her frantic look toward the door.

"No one will discover us, Miss Bingley. I shall say my piece and then leave."

"You have nothing to say to me, other than to apologize."

With defiance she lifted her chin, not willing to back down. She knew he would never harm her physically and other than that one near kiss... No. She would not dwell on that. He was a cad, a despicable cad, fooling people with his act of being a caring man of God.

"You deny that you attempted to compromise Mr. Darcy

at the stables?"

"Yes!"

His left eyebrow arched at her emphatic answer.

"I witnessed you hiding in the stable when Mr. Darcy was in attendance, so I respectfully disagree with your reply."

Her sole dedication for three years had been to attain a marriage proposal from Mr. Darcy and she could see why Lord Nathan thought she'd followed him to the stables. No one seemed to recognize she no longer held those expectations.

"Please allow me a moment to comprehend your motives," she challenged. "You drag me into the library, unescorted, to chastise me about alleged attempts to not only compromise Mr. Darcy, but the Marquis of Dorchester as well? You are full of rich irony, Lord Nathan."

"Enlighten me then as to why you crept so stealthily from the ballroom."

"Crept? I have never crept anywhere in my life, even as a child." Granted, she'd made sure no one noticed her withdrawing from the overcrowded room, exception being the annoying man standing before her, but that certainly did not qualify as creeping.

"I recall a certain incident in the stable. Had you forgotten that?"

"That is old news, Lord Nathan and we are not talking about it again." A thought crossed her mind. How, in such a crush of people, had he witnessed her slip away? "Were you spying on me?" she asked, her eyes narrowing.

"Not spying, merely interested when I noticed you leave shortly after the Marquis exited the room."

"Where I go and what I do is none of your business. You

are not my keeper."

He pressed closer and her breath almost stuttered to a complete stop. Idly, he lifted his hand and curled the hair that spilled over her shoulder around his finger.

"Maybe I should be appointed as your keeper. You could use some direction in life."

"And you have a wealth of experience in advising decent young woman?"

He cupped her chin with long, lean fingers and swept his thumb across her lower lip. Unbidden warmth spread beneath her skin as she recalled the last time they'd crossed respectable boundaries. She turned her head, her eyelids fluttering down.

That one movement was her undoing. With eyes tightly closed, her other senses took over and his utterly male fragrance danced beneath her nose. Crisp and clean with a hint of shaving cream and sandalwood. No man had ever stood so close, his very nearness created a shocking intimacy and her heart thrummed with anticipation of his next advance.

"I have a wealth of experience in ways you could not begin to fathom. I was a Rake, Miss Bingley, a man who thought nothing of seducing little girls like you." The heat of his breath brushed the shell of her ear and his fingers continued to toy with her lock of hair. "I would sweep them into my arms and kiss them until nothing existed for them except me."

Without thought she turned her head back toward him and their lips inadvertently touched for one searing second. He recoiled as though burned and stepped back to a respectable distance. Instantly she missed the heat of his body and fought a strange desire to boldly follow his retreat, to press her body against his.

"Please forgive me. My actions are unconscionable," he forced through stiff lips.

Anger and pride fought for purchase of her feelings. As he turned to leave the room, anger won the day and she called out to him in her most haughty voice.

"Who are you to say these things to me?"

Slowly he faced her, his grey eyes turning the color of frosty steel.

"My actions once again contradict my character. You may choose not to believe what I say, but I am a man who prays you find your path to happiness and contentment." He turned to walk away and then, as if he'd had another thought, turned around. "Take care who you entice with your beauty and wealth. The next man to find you alone in a hallway may take more from you than one kiss."

He executed a tight bow and exited. It wasn't until after he left the room that she realized she still held her fingers against her lips because they felt as though they'd been branded.

~~~ooo0ooo~~~

After a night of tossing and turning, sleeping only fitfully, Caroline took her time walking to the breakfast room, allowing her mind to travel where it willed. Inevitably, it chose the path that led straight to Lord Nathan.

She sighed and then chided herself. That's all she seemed to do this morning, at regular intervals, as though she had scheduled them. What on earth was wrong with her? She shook her head, already knowing the answer. She would not think of him. Not again, and sighed.

The clock chimed the ninth hour as she turned toward the

breakfast room. With luck, someone other than the Bennet ladies would be in attendance. She desperately needed more conversation than ribbons, hats and red-coated officers of the militia. As luck would have it, Georgiana was already seated. With relief she noted there was no one else in the bright, hexagonal shaped room.

"Good morning, Georgiana." Caroline made her way to where four chafing dishes awaited. She moved down the sideboard, preparing her plate.

"Good morning, Caroline," Georgiana replied and dropped a dollop of clotted cream onto her scone.

She had an air of excitement about her and kept glancing toward the door, as though expecting someone. For a brief moment Caroline's heart skipped a beat, wondering if Lord Nathan may join them, but discarded the idea as quickly as it arose. He was not a guest at Pemberley, therefore would not be breaking his fast with any of them. Not that she wanted him to see him again. She sighed.

She'd just settled at the table when Darcy joined them.

"Good morning, Fitz." Georgiana's excitement seemed to reach fever pitch and Caroline was reminded of a golden retriever pup from her childhood, forever wiggling and scrambling, waiting for someone, anyone, to throw a stick to chase.

"Good morning, Georgiana. Miss Bingley." He moved down the sideboard and prepared his own plate before joining them. A footman carefully poured them both a cup of tea before retreating back against the damask clad wall.

"May I ask her now?"

"Georgiana, maybe Miss Bingley would like to break her

fast before you pounce with your idea." Although his voice sounded stern, Caroline noted a glint of humor in his hazel eyes.

"I do believe I am capable of eating and conversing at the same time," Caroline said, and added a lump of sugar to her tea." I have been given to understand it's an acceptable activity at the dining table, as long as I do not talk with food in my mouth. Kings and Queens have been doing it for years, I am told."

"I forgot what a wit you are, Miss Bingley," came Darcy's droll response. "You may wish to revisit that observation after my sister has spoken with you."

"Once I have had my requisite cup of tea, I can face anything." She afforded a small wink at Georgiana, who readily smiled at her in return.

She enjoyed this comradery. For so long she'd relentlessly pursued Darcy and never relaxed in his company. Also, for the past year, most of their conversations, or rather her extraneous monologues had been to vilify Miss Elizabeth Bennet. No wonder he'd avoided her presence. She'd been a veritable shrew. Now, confident in her new tentative friendship with Elizabeth as well as Georgiana, she rather enjoyed this informal tête-à-tête.

The young woman managed to wait until the last drop of tea had been drunk and her plates whisked away before she broached the subject that had her feet tapping beneath the table in nervousness.

"Now, darling Georgiana," she said after daintily dabbing the corner of her mouth with a linen napkin. "What has you in such a dither?"

Darcy lifted his newspaper higher and hid behind it. That he did not want to interfere yet wanted to be in the room when his sister posed her question was irrefutable and she wondered what the two of them had cooked up.

"Miss Bingley – Caroline – as you know my companion, Mrs. Annesley has been called to care for her dear mother and we do not know when she'll return. I wondered... I mean, I'd like..." She trailed off and glanced at the newspaper Darcy still held. "Help me, Fitz."

He lowered half the newspaper and levelled a firm look at her. "Oh no, poppet, this is your request." The paper went back up in front of his face.

Georgiana fidgeted for a few seconds more, then said in one big rush, "Would you be my guest, here at Pemberley, until Fitz and Elizabeth return from their wedding trip?"

Completely flummoxed, Caroline stared at Georgiana, and then remembered to close her mouth which she was sure had fallen open in surprise. Gaping at the breakfast table was not exactly genteel. Of all things she could have imagined, and she had imagined a lot in her life, this had never crossed her mind. She would not have to leave Pemberley and be tossed on the street by Louisa. At least, not yet.

"This is a surprise, Georgiana," she replied slowly, her mind scampering in a dozen different directions. "May I give you my answer later in the day?"

She longed to say yes right away, and although her heart leaped with joy at having a reprieve from worrying about where she would lay her head, she needed to think about this proposition most thoroughly.

"Oh yes, Miss – Caroline. I shall await your answer."

Georgiana gave her an unguarded smile, the first one she'd seen in over a year. "I do hope you'll say yes."

"Mmmm… Well…" Her mind took a different tack. By staying at Pemberley, she would also be in close proximity to Lord Nathan. She placed the linen napkin on the table, unaware she'd twisted it completely out of shape. "I shall go check on my vicar; she should be awake by now."

"Do not you mean your sister?"

She frowned at Georgiana's strange question. Wasn't that what she just said? She could not be sure, but she thought she heard the stuffy Mr. Darcy harrumph. How odd.

Caroline knocked on the door to Louisa and Robert's suite. Lately, her sister had a hard time rising in the morning, complaining of severe nausea and an inability to keep anything down save weak tea and stale crackers.

Slowly she opened the door and was greeted by the sight of Louisa still in her bed, her nightcap slightly askew. Her pallid complexion confirmed that she'd had another difficult morning. Although her sister had spitefully told her she was no longer welcome in her home, it hurt Caroline's heart to see Louisa in such dire straits. She pulled a chair closer to the bed and sat.

"I wish there was something I could do for you."

"Would you carry this child for me?" Despite her weakened condition, Louisa smiled.

"That would require me to have a husband, of which the choices are few and far between, plus, I have not been asked."

"Do not worry, my dear sister. We shall soon return to London and in a few months the Season begins. I am sure there's a nice Baron or knighted gentleman who would love to have you for his wife." Louisa picked up a cracker and bit into it, grimacing as she chewed.

"Have you forgotten?"

"Forgotten what?"

"You informed me, in no uncertain terms, I was no longer welcome at your home. You wanted my suite of rooms for the nursery."

Louisa set down the cracker and tears formed in her eyes. Weeping easily had become another small foible of her pregnancy.

"Of course, you'll remain with us until you marry. I was grouchy and angry for reasons I do not remember when I said that. Can you forgive me?"

"Yes, but I may not return immediately."

Louisa stopped with a cracker half way to her mouth.

"Whatever do you mean?"

"Miss Darcy has invited me to be her guest while Darcy is away on his wedding trip. She wishes me to remain until they return."

"Does this mean you won't be with me to prepare for the baby?"

Dismayed, Caroline realized she'd never given the baby a single thought. What kind of sister was she?

"Of course, I shall be there for you. They only plan to travel for three months and there's plenty of time before your newest addition arrives."

"Oh, Caroline," Louisa reached for her hands, her red rimmed eyes brimming with fresh tears. "I do not know if I could go through this without you by my side. You are always so level headed and keep me centered."

Mild shock held her still. Never once in all her life had her sister given such a compliment. She knew she was the more forthright of the two of them, but to be thought of in this manner by her elder sister brought a strange tightness to her chest.

Louisa hiccupped back a sob and right then, she hugged her sister close, indulging in a few happy tears herself. Once again, she found herself in need of the Steward of the Linen Cupboard and fervently wished Charles were there to complete their tight little circle.

Chapter Thirteen

Nathan sat in his favorite chair, his bible opened to the Book of Psalms on his knee, dawn breaking over the eastern sky. He found himself commiserating with David over his actions at the ball with Miss Bingley.

Have mercy on me, O God, according to thy lovingkindness: according to the multitude of thy tender mercies blot out my transgression, and further down, *Create in me a clean heart; and renew a right spirit within me.* He prayed God would help mend the rift between him and Miss Bingley as once again, he'd taken the wrong tac with her.

When she slipped out of the ball room not long after the Marquis of Dorchester had exited through that very same archway, he'd been blinded by jealous rage and in a fit of temper stormed after her and accused her attempting to compromise not only the Marquis, but Darcy as well.

If she never spoke to him again, he had no one to blame but himself. He settled his head on the back of the chair and looked up to the ceiling. "Lord, help me. If she is the one You have brought me, to be my wife and help mate, give me the words to build a bridge over this chasm I have created through jealousy and pride. I cannot do this by myself."

He stayed silent for a few moments, meditating on God and committing his ways to the gentle hand of the One who loved him more than anything in this world. After reading a few more chapters, he became restless and decided to take Thunder for a ride.

Twenty minutes later, Nathan reined his horse in at the top of the hill and looked back over Pemberley estate. This was one of the things he truly enjoyed with his enviable position as Darcy's vicar. Other than his home, Adborough Hall, there was no lovelier place to live.

A light blanket of fog floated atop the meadow, destined to be burned off when the late autumn sun rose to its zenith. Spirals of smoke drifted upward in lazy curls from the multitude of chimneys scattered over the vast roof of the great house. With the wedding only two days away, Darcy's house was filled to the rafters with family and guests. One of those guests kept intruding into his thoughts and disturbing his peace of mind. What had he been thinking when they were in the music room? His actions belied his deeply held belief of honor and respect.

He leaned forward in the saddle, the leather creaking with his movement and patted the stallion's neck. "I am over my head, Thunder. How can I tell her of God's unfailing love if I cannot even be in the same room as her without wanting to kiss her?"

He sat back in the saddle and clicked his tongue in the back of his throat. At that slight command, Thunder began to trot down the hill toward a lush valley. This was a familiar trail which Thunder knew well and Nathan allowed his mind to wander.

He'd almost reached the path that would lead back to Kympton when a slight figure, dressed in a figure-hugging hunter green riding habit atop a familiar tan horse, burst through the ring of trees at a reckless pace. Valiantly, Miss Bingley attempted to bring her horse under control, but the filly paid no heed and commenced to run at a full gallop across the meadow. Another horse and rider, wearing Darcy colors, broke out of the trees after her. He recognized Daniel, one of the stable hands used to escort ladies when they rode the grounds. Daniel was too far behind to catch her, but Nathan wasn't.

He immediately urged his stallion to intercept, its long strides quickly gaining ground on the smaller horse. When he was able, he pulled alongside and grabbed the halter and between him and Thunder, brought them all to a safe stop.

"Miss Bingley, are you all right?" He maintained control of the halter in case her horse decided to bolt again.

"Yes, quite all right." She sounded breathless and her cheeks had a healthy glow from all the exercise. "You may release the halter. I am sure Lady Bess has run her course."

"May I enquire as to what happened?"

"I am not sure. Something spooked her because without warning she began to gallop. Thank goodness she stayed to the trail. I am not sure what would have happened if she'd veered into the trees."

By this time Daniel had reached them. He jumped off his horse and approached, deep concern etched on his face.

"Are you all right, Miss?" He ran an experienced eye over

the horse's form.

"Yes, thank you, Daniel."

"Do you mind if we stop here for a moment. I want to check her out, make sure she wasn't injured or anything." Nathan asked.

"Please do. I'd hate for Bess to have been injured. I enjoy riding her whenever I am here." She leaned forward and caressed the horse's silky mane. "She's been a good friend. Have not you, Bess?"

The horse nickered and tossed back her head as if in agreement. He dismounted Thunder and quickly ran his hands over Bess' flank and checked her hooves while Daniel held the halter and spoke soothing words. Nothing seemed untoward, until he spotted a slight burr, stuck beneath the cinch halter that encircled her belly. He removed the prickly irritant and came around to Miss Bingley's side.

"Here's your culprit," he said, holding up the burr. "Easy to pick up when you're traveling through the woods. You can let her go, Daniel. I do not think she'll take off again."

He tossed the burr aside and quickly mounted Thunder. Daniel released Bess' halter and remounted his horse.

"May I join you? I was finishing my ride and taking the trail back to Kympton."

"Ride where you please, Lord Nathan." She gave the reins a quick flick and Bess began a soft trot down the path. "I do not own the trails of Pemberley any more than you."

It was obvious that she remained in a fit of pique over their encounter at the ball, and she had every right. He'd behaved in a high-handed and judgmental manner. How could he expect her to believe God forgives all sins when he could not see past his own jealousy and forgive her?

"You may go back to Pemberley, Daniel. I'll escort Miss Bingley from here."

"Good enough, guvner." Daniel tipped his hat and with a firm hand turned his horse around and headed back to Pemberley's stables.

Nathan nudged Thunder ahead and came alongside Caroline. She kept her eyes forward, the tilt of her chin letting him know that she was not conceding anything to him. At least not right now, although he suspected she had some kind of tendre for him.

"Miss Bingley, I apologized after our uncomfortable incident—"

"Incident? Is that what we are calling it now?

Blast it all, he'd put his foot in it again. At one time he may have been able to read the nuances of a woman's psyche, but then, they'd been as debauched as he. A crook of his eyebrow brought a majority of women to his side, and although he'd taunted her with the thought that he'd seduced innocent young women, nothing could be further from the truth. He'd made sure to avoid the prim and proper young misses like a healthy man avoids a plague-ridden city.

He brought Thunder in front of her horse, forcing her to stop. This seemed to be a replay of his actions in the stable and did not make him any more comfortable, but he wished to speak with her in a forthright manner.

"In no way do I minimize my behavior. I treated you with complete disdain and can only blame myself. You behaved with perfect manners and have done nothing to be ashamed."

She gave an elegant sniff yet refused to look at him.

He sighed deeply. How could he reach her and achieve forgiveness?

"Miss Bingley, I hold you in high regard. You intrigue me and for that reason I find myself looking for you in the crowd. I'd like us to begin again and be friends."

She finally faced him and held his gaze.

"You look for me in the crowd?"

"Yes, Miss Bingley," he said with a slight smile. "I look for you in the crowd. How else would I have noticed you leave the ballroom? It was an absolute crush."

A secretive smile crossed her lips, so quickly he'd have missed it had he not been watching so close. "I thought as much," she whispered, sounding a bit triumphant.

She stared off into the meadow, as if measuring her thoughts, before glancing back at him. He knew she'd come to a decision and hoped, nay prayed, she'd accept the olive branch he'd extended.

"I accept your apology Lord Nathan and you might do me the courtesy of not believing I am the blackguard others paint my character as. There are two sides to every story and one day, if I come to trust you, I shall tell you mine."

With that, she lightly kicked Bess and moved around his horse, leaving Nathan to follow.

For a few minutes he enjoyed the view of Miss Bingley riding Bess. Her riding habit of deep hunter green fit her figure most lovingly and her trim hat, accented with deep purple, was perched jauntily atop her braided hair. He decided to bridge the gap between them and start a pleasant conversation. With that in mind, he brought Thunder up alongside her.

"Miss Bingley, other than the 'incident' – she snorted

inelegantly and he grinned – did you enjoy the ball?"

She paused for so long he wondered if she planned on ignoring him the whole ride back to Pemberley. At long last she answered.

"There were moments that were truly enjoyable. Your brother is an excellent dancer and a fine gentleman. He treated me with the utmost respect, for which I am truly grateful."

He was reminded of the behavior of Viscount Stanhope and felt his anger rise again.

"There were others who were most unjust toward you. I regret taking you anywhere near that man," he bit out, curbing harsher words he'd like to express.

"Viscount Stanhope only voiced what many people whispered throughout the night. They seem to think because I am from 'trade' I am deaf to their conversations. Darcy will bear the brunt of most of their disdain, but I am sure he was well aware of this before he proposed to Elizabeth."

"Stanhope is vulgar and rude. If I were your family or betrothed, I would have called him out for the vile things he suggested."

"But then, you are neither, so the point is moot."

"What would you say if I wished to change that?"

The words were out of his mouth before he could stop them. The tightening of her hands on the reins let him know she was equally surprised. They rode in silence as he waited for her response.

"Given the propensity of you misconstruing my intentions, I wish you to clarify that comment," she said carefully.

"I have never——" He bit back the argument he'd have

given. She was right in her assumption; he did jump to conclusions with her.

Intellectually, she challenged him, more than any other lady of his acquaintance. In comparison, his relationship with Miss Tattersall had been quite colorless, lacking the thrust and parry of unfettered opinions and he appreciated the fact Miss Bingley did not seem to hold back when she was frustrated, angry or even sad.

"You intrigue me. I find myself thinking of things we could discuss when, and if we should meet. Your opinions matter to me, which I find quite refreshing."

"You value my opinion? Then why do you chastise me every time we meet?"

"I find it frustrating that you see society for what it is and yet you pine to become one with it. Given your wealth and the few necessary connections you have, I am surprised you would allow yourself to become someone's wife solely for the use of your fortune."

"I would expect my husband to respect me. To value my opinion, such as you say you do."

"Miss Bingley, this is where the fairy tale ends. If you were successful and managed to gain the attention of a titled gentleman, you most likely would be unsuccessful in retaining his affection."

"I disagree. There are many stories of noble men marrying women who were not from titled families."

He clenched his jaw in frustration. She refused to see the hard facts, making him wonder if she'd read one too many romantic novels that had become so popular in recent years. It was time she saw life through a clear pane and not one so rose colored.

"What you say is true, although marriages between the social spheres are becoming more frequent, very few of them are what you might term as a love match. Many from the *ton* have exhausted their wealth, some through bad investments, most through self-indulgent ways, and are forced to wed an heiress to save their ancestral homes."

"I never thought you'd be so cynical. These are your people."

"Not cynical, only a realist. Once the requisite heir is born, most of these 'noble' men live in Town, carrying on as though they were unencumbered, leaving the controversial wife in the country. Are you sure you wish such a life?"

"I'd not stay in the country. I would expect to continue living in Town, as I do now."

He cut a sideways glance to see for himself if she truly believed that statement. She was not smiling, nor did it look as though she teased him. He reigned in his horse and she followed suit, turning to face him.

"Miss Bingley, have you forgotten you become your husband's property once married? All your wealth becomes his, unless otherwise directed in the marriage agreement. You become his chattel. If he wishes you to stay in the country, there you shall remain."

"That's untenable."

"That's the bleak, hard truth."

Lady Bess huffed and pawed the ground, as if sensing the rising agitation from her rider. Caroline chewed her lip, deep in thought and then raised her gaze to his.

"Would you behave in such a manner?"

His breath caught at the raw emotion in her emerald eyes. This woman deserved to be loved for herself, not for worldly gain.

"No, but then, I am not in need of an heiress. When I marry, my wife will be an equal partner, one who shares my desire to serve and she will be cherished. I intend to honor my wife and as the Book of Proverbs states, *her children will rise up and call her blessed, her husband also, and he praises her*."

He could not be sure, because she looked away so quickly, but her eyes took on a sudden sheen, as though filled with unshed tears.

"I think you'll make a wonderful husband," she whispered. She flicked the reins and surged ahead. All conversation ended as this part of the trail cut through the dense woods and they had to ride single file.

Chapter Fourteen

One single question – *What would you say if I wished to change that?* – looped through her thoughts. It wasn't a complete declaration, but the fact he looked for her in the crowd told her clearly if he wasn't in love with her now, he was well on his way. She could not stop a smile from spreading across her face as she rode ahead of Lord Nathan, anticipation making her heart race.

She was grateful they had to ride single file, at least for another half mile as it gave her time to think. What would she do if he proposed? Marriage to Lord Nathan meant setting aside her long sought-after goal of living amongst Society's elite. Yes, he was the son of a Duke, but he'd eschewed living in Town many years ago and that would not change after marriage.

She relived the moment he'd stood so close their breath mingled, how she'd wanted him to place his arms around her and draw her closer. Physically, she was attracted to him and knew they would enjoy each other's company, but on the other side of that coin were their debates and arguments. He did state her opinions mattered to him, that he thought of things they could discuss.

She gave an inelegant snort and Bess huffed out one as well.

"You are so right, Lady Bess," she whispered. "Lord Nathan and I have yet to discuss anything without it devolving into an argument and me storming off in anger."

"Did you say something, Miss Bingley?" Lord Nathan called to her.

"No, I am discussing politics with Lady Bess," she threw over her shoulder and was rewarded by a soft chuckle coming from behind.

"Ah...I see. Rest assured that I make it a policy to never come between a lady and her horse as they discuss politics."

"At times, Lord Nathan, you are a wise man."

"I am learning, Miss Bingley. I am learning." The path widened and he cantered up alongside her. "Did Lady Bess have any insights you care to share?"

She slid a glance sideways at him, noting his ready smile and how his grey eyes no longer looked like storm clouds. Instead, they sparkled with humor.

"You, Lord Nathan," she said in a faux haughty voice, "are not privy to our private conversations. Lady Bess stated, quite categorically, she is exclusive with whom she speaks."

"She did, did she?" He looked straight ahead, a smile tugging at his firm mouth.

"Yes, although she gave me leave to advise that you are welcome to bring her apples."

Now he outright laughed and she was hard put not to smile along with him.

"Then, I shall have to ensure that when I attend

Pemberley, I bring along some kind of treat for all the ladies I might visit."

Her breath caught at the back of her throat. She did not dare look at him, afraid of what she might find. It sounded as though he... flirted with her, but she'd been mistaken more than once when it came to the male species. She refused to rise to his comment and urged Bess into a quicker pace.

The path wound alongside the trees and continued through the meadow leading to Pemberley. Daniel greeted them when they entered the small courtyard outside the stable and helped her dismount before leading Lady Bess into the stable.

"Thank you for escorting me back to Pemberley, Lord Nathan." She gave him a small curtsy and turned to enter the stable. She made a point of brushing Lady Bess herself after a ride, using that time to quiet her thoughts and today she had many things to ponder.

"Miss Bingley," Lord Nathan called after her before she disappeared inside the building. "May I call on you later this afternoon?"

Startled, she froze in place and almost forgot to breathe. Turning slowly, she looked up at him, disconcerted to see an expression she could not quite decipher. Knowing he needed an answer, she took a much-needed breath.

"Yes, you may. We will be having tea around two of the clock this afternoon."

"Until then." He tipped his hat and pulled on the reins to turn his horse around. She stood and watched him canter down the drive until he rounded the corner and disappeared.

Long, slow strokes of the brush across Lady Bess's coat soothed the turmoil of her mind. Did Lord Nathan mean to court her? She may have read too much into their conversation, but everything seemed to point toward that very thing.

Lady Bess bumped her soft nose against her shoulder when the brush stilled as more turbulent thoughts fought for attention.

"I am sorry, Bess. I have a lot to think about."

She continued brushing, murmuring small nonsense to the gentle mare while her mind raced.

Was she ready to lend aid to a husband who ministered to those with so little? She thought back to Miss Braithwaite, who'd thanked Lord Nathan effusively for something as simple as broth for a sick woman. At the time she remembered her heart being touched by the humble response from Lord Nathan. There had been no lavish bowing and scraping, complimenting only to receive something in return. He genuinely wished to extend the love of God to his parishioners through service.

Could she, Caroline Bingley, lower herself to serve others? Could she be the wife he needed?

"Oh, Bess." She laid her forehead on Bess's shoulder. "He confuses me greatly. In between compliments and flirtatious comments, he continues to chastise me. Is this what our marriage would be like?" She stepped back and continued to brush out the mane. "If so, then I am not sure I would accept."

Once Bess was properly brushed down and situated in her stall, she made her way to the house. She had about four hours before Lord Nathan joined them for tea. Her thoughts continued to swirl and she longed for someone in whom she could confide. Someone who would not judge.

"God, if you can hear me, please send someone I can trust," she whispered fervently.

She turned the corner and almost ran into Elizabeth.

"Caroline. You must have gotten up early to get in a ride already."

"Yes, there are times when a little solitude helps clear my mind."

"I could not agree with you more, it's one of the reasons I walk so much. Not only for exercise, but for a chance to clear the cobwebs from my mind."

"You were going to read, I shan't bother you then…" She noticed Elizabeth held a small book in her hand.

"Nonsense, you are not a bother. I am only returning this before breaking my fast. Have you eaten?"

"No. I wanted to ride first."

"Then I look forward to you joining me in the breakfast room."

They parted ways and Caroline continued on to her room. Lucy waited patiently for her and quickly helped her change and freshen up. She dressed her in one of her new day dresses from Mrs. Braxton. With plans to remain at Pemberley for another three months, she'd placed a few more orders and looked forward to wearing them.

Within fifteen minutes, she entered the breakfast room and acknowledged Elizabeth before preparing her plate and sitting across from her new, unexpected friend. Could this be the person God sent in answer to her prayer? She could not help the smile that crossed her lips at the irony of the situation. The one woman she'd despaired over was now seated across from her, soon to be a part of her extended family.

"What do you find so amusing, Caroline?"

She glanced up and caught the merry twinkle in Elizabeth's eyes. At one time this would have annoyed her greatly, but her heart was changing, bit by bit, and now she could see humor where before she saw fault.

"I was marveling at the two of us enjoying our time together instead of looking for ways to end it."

Elizabeth laughed out loud and set down her tea cup. "That is true. Your character has changed much since last year. I like this Caroline Bingley. She has much to offer society."

"May I confide something to you?"

A hint of wariness crossed Elizabeth's features, but she straightened in her chair and said, "I am not sure if I am someone you should share confidences with. Could not your sister—"

"No," she interjected. "I asked God for guidance and He sent me you. At first, I was surprised, but given the path you and Darcy have taken, it makes complete sense."

"How is that?" Elizabeth's brow furrowed as she listened.

"You and Darcy had an uncommon courtship, beset by prejudices on both sides."

"That is true," Elizabeth murmured.

"Lord Nathan has been speaking to me, not always in a conciliatory manner." She noted the quick smile Elizabeth tried to hide. "He upbraids me for my quest to marry well and we often argue the point. In fact, we argue almost all the time. He's quite frustrating."

"My dear Caroline, you sound like Mr. Darcy and I. We got off on the wrong foot from the first time we met at the

Assembly in Meryton. Do you recall that night?"

"I do. I was absolutely horrid to everyone there, even my own party."

"Hmmm… well, yes you were, but that is in the past. You are quite forgiven."

"Thank you. How did you and Darcy get off on the wrong foot? I scarcely recall him speaking to you."

Elizabeth leaned over the table, as if imparting a great secret. "Your brother encouraged him to ask me to dance and he said, 'She is tolerable, but not handsome enough to tempt me'." She imitated Darcy's manner and voice as she relayed the occurrence.

"No!" Caroline was aghast, but could very well imagine Darcy saying such a thing. He hated public assemblies and meeting new people who only looked upon him for his wealth.

"Yes. Our courtship was doomed because the very next day I told all and sundry that I could have easily forgiven his pride if he had not mortified mine."

She laughed outright at Elizabeth's pert response to Darcy's dreadful behavior. It was a small miracle they'd found each other as it was obvious to anyone who spent any time in their company saw a deep and abiding love.

"Oh, Elizabeth, you allow me have hope."

"You have feelings for Lord Nathan?"

Caroline pushed the eggs around on the plate with her fork and thought about Elizabeth's question. She had feelings. Copious amounts of feelings, not all of them charitable, but there were moments when she desired him more than she thought possible. All other men paled in comparison to him, even her beloved Darcy. She no longer looked at him in the same manner.

Finally, she lifted her gaze to find Elizabeth studying her closely.

"I have feelings for him, and I believe he is going to ask permission to court me."

"And you have reservations about this?"

"Yes... No." She contemplated the brilliant blue sky through the window, gathering her thoughts. "I had such great plans for my life." She turned her face back to Elizabeth. "But, as you know, they did not come to fruition."

Elizabeth gave her a small nod of agreement, but did not interrupt.

"Lord Nathan challenges me to be a better person. His wife will be expected to aid him with his parishioners, to give more than she's capable of..." she trailed off into a whisper.

Tears pooled in her eyes and threatened to fall into her lap. Elizabeth rose from her chair and came around to touch her shoulder.

"A year ago, if anyone asked me if you were capable of compassion, I would have said 'No' with complete conviction, but it is obvious to me, as well as Mr. Darcy, that you have changed. The woman you are becoming is not only beautiful on the outside, but also acquiring a beauty within. Do not doubt yourself. You have much to offer Lord Nathan. You have your heart, which is far more precious that money and jewels."

"Thank you." She stood and threw impulsive arms around Elizabeth's shoulders. After a brief hesitation, Elizabeth returned the hug. "I am so glad we are family."

"I am too," Elizabeth replied, her tone somewhat bemused and she stepped out of the hug. "I must not tarry. Mama's nerves are wearing her down and I promised to bring her a tea."

Caroline bade her goodbye and sat down to finish her meal although not much left the plate as her appetite had dissipated. Thoughts about Lord Nathan, what Elizabeth shared and her own indecision plagued her.

Later that day...

"Caroline, are you all right?" Georgiana looked at her in concern.

"Yes." She picked up her tea cup and then placed it back onto the matching saucer and glanced at the clock on the fireplace mantle. Nearly ten minutes had gone by since the clock chimed two times.

"You have been glancing at the clock for almost twenty minutes now."

"I have?"

She toyed with the idea of taking a bite of her cucumber sandwich, but knew she'd never be able to swallow anything given how tight her nerves were stretched. Instead, she picked up her embroidery hoop, intending to focus on the rose she'd started earlier. Louisa entered the salon and sat in the chair next to Georgiana.

"Thank goodness. I have been longing for a good cup of tea."

The two ladies launched into a discussion of different teas, but Caroline heard none of it because framed in the door stood Lord Nathan. He gave each of the ladies a polite bow and then fixed his attention upon her.

"Miss Bingley, would you take a walk with me in the

garden." He waved his arm in the direction of the yard through the French doors of the parlor they were seated in.

She hesitated and knew the moment she dreaded yet anticipated had arrived. With a heart that threatened to flop out of her chest, she set down her embroidery, stood and smoothed the front of her skirt with trembling hands. After settling a shawl about her shoulders, she preceded him through the doors, very aware of his large hand resting so intimately against the small of her back. What would her sister and Georgiana make of his overt familiarity? She walked a little faster, evading his familiar touch and turned to face him at the end of the terrace.

"You presume too much, Lord Nathan. As stated before, I am not your betrothed, nor am I your sister."

"That's what I have struggled with."

He paced to the edge of the terrace and stood by the balustrade, hands clasped behind his back. His attention seemed centered on the partially frozen lake bordering the expanse of the garden. She drew her shawl closer around her body and waited for him to continue. Finally, when she thought her lips would turn blue from cold, he faced her.

"I tried not to love you, but it has been difficult."

Her breath caught and a flock of butterflies took flight in her stomach. He loved her? This man who chastised her every chance, loved her?

"You captivated my heart from the moment I met you. I have prayed and sought God for answers because you were more earthly minded than heavenly and you only sought a marriage that would elevate you in society. You held no regard for whom you would marry, but what you would marry."

He stood in front of her and drew her icy hands into his large warm ones. She did not pull away, although her heart ached over his cataloguing of her past faults. All of them true. She was startled out of her melancholy when he brought her cold bare hands up to his lips and kissed each one.

"And then, dear Miss Bingley, you gave me hope where I had none before. You may not realize this, but you are a new creation in Christ. It's there in your countenance, in your speech; I daresay it's in your walk. You exude a peace which was not there before and you smile more readily. Georgiana practically glows from the friendship you bestow upon her."

"I… I do not know what to say." His words rang of truth and she knew everything in her life had changed. Once she'd whispered that prayer to her grandmother and sought out the Lord at Kympton parish, her whole being felt as though a heavy load had fallen from her shoulders.

"Say that you will allow me court you properly and after a suitable time, I estimate three weeks, marry me."

She focused on their clasped hands. Since they'd parted that morning, her thoughts had been consumed by questions of whether she was prepared to be a vicar's wife, caring for others, tending those who had less alongside her husband? Was she prepared for Mr. Darcy to be her patron and by proxy, Elizabeth her patroness?

Dear Lord, what is my answer?

If she refused him, he would walk away and she'd return to London. Her dull future stretched before her filled with 'what if's' and 'might have's'. With clarity she knew, she just knew, this was what she wanted. She did not need the approval of Society as long as she had this man by her side. He was her future.

She raised her gaze to his and almost broke into tears at the love that shone through his eyes.

"Yes. I'll marry you, Mr. Kerr."

He cupped her face in his large hands and brought his closer. She rose to meet his kiss, but he paused and whispered, "May I kiss you, Miss Bingley?"

Her heart soared and she whispered back, against lips that were but a hair's breadth from her. "Yes."

"Thank God." He crushed her lips to his, angling his head to deepen the kiss and she lost all sense of time. The cold which earlier threatened to seep into her bones, retreated in the midst of his embrace. In three weeks she'd be Mrs. Nathan Kerr.

"We cannot get married!" She cried out, breaking from the embrace and stumbling away.

"What are you talking about?" He ran a hand through his unruly curls and reached for her again. She sidestepped his arms and drew her shawl close around her body. The cold was sharper now that she was no longer in his arms.

"I promised Georgiana I would stay with her while Darcy and Elizabeth are on their wedding trip, and Louisa is having her baby. I should be there for her—"

"My love," he took her cold hands in his, not releasing them when she would have pulled away. "I have your promise of marriage and although I want nothing more than to marry you immediately – Gretna Green comes to mind – I can wait until Darcy returns."

"What about Louisa? I promised to be there when the baby comes."

"Do you think I am going to lock you in the parsonage and

not allow you to see your sister, or stay with her when her time comes?"

"I do not know."

"You're honest in your answers to me, I'll give you that." He drew her close and wrapped his strong arms around her and she welcomed the warmth from his body. "I would never stop you from being with your sister. We have a lifetime to make memories."

"Yes, we do." She glanced up, admiring his strong jaw line. "After three months have gone by."

"Minx," he teased and tapped her cold nose with his finger. "This will be a good thing. I have three months to court you properly."

"I like the sound of that, and I have three months to find out what you like and dislike."

He adjusted her shawl so that it covered her shoulders again and offered his arm to escort her back into the house. A flurry of movement by the window told her Georgiana and Louisa were most likely scrambling back to their seats. She hid a smile, knowing they'd witnessed her most joyous moment.

"Just so you know," he said as they strolled toward the French doors, "I like the color green, because it reminds me of a fine pair of eyes" – she blushed – "and a roast beef dinner with Yorkshire pudding."

"Not fair! I was to discover this on my own." She stepped ahead of him after he'd opened the door. "I shan't give away my secrets. You will have a project."

"I look forward to discovering everything about you." He whispered in her ear, causing her to tremble, and not from cold.

They entered the parlor and Georgiana and Louisa studiously kept their attention on their activities. Georgiana her embroidery and Louisa her reading, although the book Louisa held was upside down, which caused Lord Nathan to smile quite broadly.

They both looked up with innocent expressions when he approached and gave them both a small bow.

"I take my leave, ladies and look forward to seeing all of you at church tomorrow."

The look he sent Caroline's way held much promise and he strode out of the room. Both Georgiana and Louisa watched as she sank into the chair and sighed.

"Well?" Louisa finally broke the silence.

"He says he loves me and wishes to court me, we have come to an understanding."

Louisa put down the book, arose from the chair and hugged her. Georgiana also cried out, "I am so happy for you."

"I want you to know, Louisa, Mr. Kerr wishes me to be with you when it's your time."

"I will admit, this would have worried me. He's a good man."

"Oh, he's the best, Mrs. Hurst. Our parishioners love him, and I am sure they will come to love Caroline as well." Georgiana looked at Caroline, dismay filling her eyes. "What about staying at Pemberley? No, no. Do not worry. I shouldn't be so selfish."

"Georgiana, please do not distress yourself. We discussed this and I am staying with you as planned, but do not be surprised if Lord Nathan comes to visit us both – a lot. You will be our chaperone. Are you up to the task?"

"Yes. I can be quite ferocious." She tinkled out a laugh. "You will become tired of my company, I am sure."

"Never." She reached across and took Georgiana's hand in hers. "You have become my friend, almost a little sister to me."

"Oh good, there's still tea." Mrs. Bennet entered the room, followed by Catherine and Mary. Georgiana rose and pulled the bell cord to request more sandwiches and a fresh pot of tea.

Mrs. Bennet settled on the couch opposite Caroline and avoided looking at her. Catherine and Mary sat on either side, although they at least afforded her a polite smile, which she returned.

Conversation quickly turned to the double wedding, only two days away and left in peace, she reflected on the happy events of the afternoon. In three months she'd become Mrs. Nathan Kerr. Such a lovely name.

~~~ooo0ooo~~~

It was with a sense of great anticipation that Nathan greeted the Lord's Day. Caroline had accepted his proposal and his heart could not contain his joy. He prepared for the Sunday Service, which would be a decidedly happy affair as this was the final reading of the banns for all interested parties from Pemberley.

Tomorrow would also be hectic as the actual ceremony would be performed by him and he knew that when he asked each couple to repeat their vows, his focus would be on his affianced, knowing that they too would soon be following in their footsteps.

"Would that day come sooner, Lord. Three months... Please grant me patience." He breathed a quick prayer as he made his way to the chapel to make sure there were enough hymnals in the pews and fresh flowers in the vestibule.

All too soon the church was full and he was finalizing his sermon, based on Second Corinthians, Chapter Thirteen, more commonly known as the Love Chapter. His choice had been deliberate. He truly believed when husbands treated their wives as Christ treated His church, and followed the precept set down in Holy Scripture, marriages were more secure and both parties more content. He vowed to hold Caroline in such esteem.

The church was quite full of family, friends and guests for the wedding as well as regular parishioners. Hymns were sung and he preached his sermon before a congregation very open to the thought of true love. Finally, he reached the end of the service where he would read the banns for the third and final time for Mr. Darcy and Mr. Bingley.

In a solemn voice he intoned, "I publish the banns of marriage between Fitzwilliam Arthur Darcy of Kympton parish, Derbyshire and Elizabeth Sophia Bennet of Longbourn parish, Hertfordshire. This is the third and final time of asking. If any of you know cause or just impediment why these two persons should not be joined together in Holy Matrimony, you are to declare it before this assembly, or forever hold your peace."

He waited for a few seconds before moving onto the next.

"I publish the banns of marriage between Charles Matthew Bingley of St. George Hanover Square parish, London and Jane Augusta Bennet of Longbourn parish, Hertfordshire. This is the third and final time of asking. If any of you know cause or just impediment why these two persons should not be joined together in Holy Matrimony, you are to declare it before this assembly, or forever hold your peace."

There was a tittering amongst the parishioners, who enjoyed the fact a joint wedding was taking place in their chapel on the morrow. Nathan waited until the soft chuckling subsided before starting again. This next announcement would shock everyone and he could not wait to view the reactions.

"Before we leave for the day and I pray the benediction, I have one more order of business." He cleared his throat and glanced down at Caroline. "I publish the banns of marriage between Lord Reverend Nathanial William Kerr of Kympton parish, Derbyshire" – several gasps rippled through the church and Mr. Darcy openly gaped. This was much more fun than expected. – "and Caroline Anastasia Bingley of St. George Hanover Square parish, London. This is the first time of asking. If any of you know cause or just impediment why these two persons should not be joined together in Holy Matrimony, you are to declare it before this assembly, or forever hold your peace."

He grinned openly as Georgiana turned in her pew and reached over, clasping Caroline's hand. Her excited whisper resonated for everyone to hear, such were the acoustics of the chapel. "I am so happy for you." Mr. Darcy, after he'd closed his mouth and taken Elizabeth's hand in his, allowed a glimmer of a smile to cross his face. Elizabeth's bright eyes sparkled with happy tears.

Charles, seated next to Jane, looked bemused. Nathan approached him yesterday out of courtesy for his sister's hand in marriage. Although Caroline was of age and could choose whom she married, he wanted to give Charles the respect that came as head of household. Jane as always remained serene.

His brother Max, and George, who'd arrived late last evening for the wedding, stoically faced forward, but wide smiles creased both their faces and he knew he'd receive a full ribbing later on in the day from both of them.

When everybody settled, he read a portion from psalms, prayed the benediction and led the happy congregation in the final hymn. He had eyes for no one but his beloved, who positively glowed in her pale-yellow muslin gown, with a contrasting chestnut brown wool spencer. Atop her glorious curls was another jaunty hat, swathed in rich silk, a single feather fixed along the side.

Impatient as he was for the three months to be over, he cherished the thought of properly courting his bride. He adored how she blushed when he snatched a stolen kiss or two. The Lord had truly blessed him.

One year later…

"I have received a letter from Charles."

"How lovely." Caroline set down the needlepoint she'd been working on, a linen handkerchief for Nathan. "What does our dear brother have to say?"

"He rambles on for quite a bit, but at least his handwriting is legible." Louisa stated with a small laugh. "Jane has been a good influence on him."

"Yes, she has," she agreed. "Do not keep me in suspense, what does he write?"

Louisa settled her new reading spectacles on her nose and scanned the letter. Although she did not read the letter in its entirety, she spoke aloud the parts that Caroline would find pertinent.

"He states he and Jane have purchased an estate not ten miles from Darcy and Elizabeth."

"That will make Elizabeth glad. I know how close she is to Jane."

"Yes, and also remove them from Mrs. Bennet. Charles writes her interference in their daily lives has become unbearable, which we knew would happen, and with a baby on the way—" Louisa lowered the letter to her lap and stared at Caroline, slack jawed.

"A baby!" Caroline cried out with joy. "Oh, they will be so happy. When does the child arrive?"

"What? Oh…" Louisa picked the letter back up and began again. "…a baby on the way, and by the time we receive this letter, they will already be moved." She glanced up at Caroline. "Mr. Darcy gave Charles sound advice there. He knew they'd want to sever ties with Longbourn and urged Charles not to buy the property in Hertfordshire." She continued reading from the letter. "The babe is expected six months hence. Oh, poor Jane. She must be absolutely exhausted from the move."

"I am sure she was. When you were expecting Nicholas, you slept the whole day away at times."

"There is much adjustment when you have a child. Your body changes in wonderful ways."

Louisa gave her a knowing look and Caroline felt her cheeks turn pink with heat.

"I won't know anything about that for a while. There are still two weeks until our wedding."

"Fortunately, Jane can attend the ceremony as she will not yet be in confinement, and they live a scant five miles from

Kympton." Louisa removed her glasses. "I believe Mr. Hurst and I should look into buying property in Derbyshire. If the whole family is going to be there, it makes sense. I want Nicholas to grow up around family and Mr. Hurst's new business venture with Mr. Darcy and Mr. Gardiner would run much smoother if we resided nearby."

"There was a time Charles would gladly have banished us all to the Hebrides, but now, I am sure he'd love for us all to be closer."

"This year has been difficult, with Nathan's aunt and uncle passing away, but your wedding day is just around the corner."

"Two more weeks. I cannot believe it's finally going to happen."

Four weeks after Nathan proposed, his Uncle Moreland and his wife Millicent were killed in a carriage accident. As he was an uncle, the mourning period lasted for six months and not a full year. Naturally the wedding had been postponed and with Louisa so close to delivering, they agreed to wait until she no longer required Caroline's help and set the date for early November.

The past few months, with Nathan so far away in Derbyshire, made her realize how much she truly loved him. The royal mail service had to have noticed an increase in the number of letters travelling between London and Derbyshire when she returned to Town. She'd gone from having no one to correspond with to spending a few hours each morning going through her letters and replying. Not only did she receive daily missives from Nathan, but letters from his mother, Georgiana, Elizabeth and Jane, and most surprisingly, Miss Braithwaite. The dear heart had practically adopted her as one of her own and sent her the most entertaining news of what was happening in Kympton.

Darcy graciously offered his home for family and friends as the ceremony was taking place in Kympton and the Archbishop himself declared he would make the journey to Derbyshire and officiate over the service.

Two weeks could not come soon enough.

~~~ooo0ooo~~~

"I, Caroline Anastasia Bingley, take thee, Nathanial William Kerr, to my wedded husband, to have and to hold from this day forward, for better for worse, for richer, for poorer, in sickness and in health, to love, cherish, and to obey, till death us do part, according to God's holy ordinance; and thereto I give thee my troth."

She waited in a heightened sense of euphoria and heard nothing more until the Archbishop uttered those long-awaited words, "I pronounce they be man and wife together." With her hand tucked safely in Nathan's she floated through the closing prayers and the reading of the psalms and it was only when the pealing of the bells began as they exited the church, all of it came at her in a mad rush.

They were finally married!

Nathan lifted her into the festive carriage and this time she relished the flex and tightening of his muscles. He sat and quickly took her hand in his, removing the ivory glove and brought her fingers to his lips. Between kissing each knuckle, he whispered. "I love you."

"And I, you, Mr. Kerr."

He cradled her face in his hands. "I am truly sorry for this, Caroline, but you are now Lady Nathanial Kerr."

She started laughing and the more she tried to stop, the harder she laughed. Nathan did not join in, as he knew not what she laughed about, but his handsome mouth tilted into a grin.

"What is so funny?" He waited until she stopped with a small hiccup.

"Dear husband. Never say God does not have a sense of humor. For years I strove to capture the interest of a Peer, any member of the *ton*, without success." She caressed his face with an affectionate hand. "And fell in love with a vicar, so far from my hopes and dreams."

She held a finger to those lips she loved so much when he would have spoken. "No, do not say anything. I am content and filled with joy in this life and now that I do not care, God deems fit to give me a title."

He chuckled at her explanation and kissed her fully on the lips. Finally, he bid the driver take them away and they both turned and waved goodbye to the cheers and well wishes of friends and family.

She looked adoringly at her husband. How she treasured that word, husband.

"I love you Nathanial William Kerr, and I do not care if we never entertain Society. I am quite content with our cozy parsonage and your parishioners."

"I am glad you say that, my lovely, beautiful wife, but do you remember the letter I received from Max's solicitor a few weeks ago, requesting I visit the old curmudgeon in London?"

She nodded assent.

"He informed me as Uncle Moreland and Aunt Millicent had no children or other direct heirs, he bequeathed his estate to me. We've become land owners, not more than twenty miles from Kympton."

"And you're only telling me now?"

"Consider this my wedding gift to you." He leaned in and kissed her softly on the lips.

"You are trying to distract me."

"Is it working?" She could feel him smile against her lips.

"Yes," she sighed and let him kiss her again. Once he pulled back, she asked. "Shouldn't the estate have gone to Max, or George?"

"No, he stipulated in his will I was to inherit. Max has Adborough Hall and George has Keswick Manor, which was part of mother's dowry."

"Does this mean you'll leave the church?"

"Yes, my darling, but not until Darcy finds a replacement, which could take a few months." He caressed her cheek with the back of his fingers. "We'll entertain guests, have copious amounts of children to carry on our legacy, and look after our own tenants as the estate is substantial. Are you prepared for that adventure?"

"I will face anything if you are with me." Happy tears of joy pooled in her eyes and she reached for her ivory reticule.

Nathan placed a hand over hers and stilled her movement. He reached inside his morning coat and brandished a newly embroidered linen handkerchief with C&N stitched on the corner above a tiny rose.

"I am ever your humble Steward of the Linen Cupboard, Lady Nathanial Kerr."

THE END

The Love Chapter

Love has patience, love is kind, not jealous, love does not boast, it is not proud, it does not dishonor, it does not seek things for itself, it does not become angry, it does not charge evil to another, it does not rejoice over unrighteousness, but rejoices together in truth: it endures all things, it believes all things, it hopes all things, it is steadfast in all things. And whether prophecies be abolished: or tongues will cease: or knowledge will be abolished: love never perishes.

I Corinthians 13: 4-8

SueBarr.ca